Praise for *Cross My Heart*
THE HIDDEN DIARY,

Cross My Heart was *very* descriptive (but not, like, overloaded!) and fun. It's a touching story that a lot of girls can relate to because of their own busy parents. I liked the mystery, too!

Lilly, eleven years old, daughter of Liz Curtis Higgs,
author of *Bad Girls of the Bible*

Mama mia! *Cross My Heart* was a great book! I liked the way the author left you hanging at the end of each chapter. It made you want to keep reading. I could really relate to some of the characters, and Claudette made me laugh. You'll love this book! Cross my heart!

Tavia, ten years old, daughter of Deborah Raney,
author of *A Vow to Cherish* and *Beneath a Southern Sky*

This book was really good, interesting, and fun. I couldn't say I had one favorite part because I loved the whole book! I couldn't put it down.

Tyler, eleven years old, daughter of Lisa E. Samson,
author of *The Church Ladies*

I couldn't put this book down! I guarantee you'll love *Cross My Heart,* and it will keep you on the edge of your seat.

Marie, thirteen years old, daughter of Terri Blackstock,
author of the NEWPOINTE 911 series

Cross My Heart is a very exciting book. Lucy . . . meets new friends and learns about God. I know my friends will love this book like I did. Maybe we'll find a hidden diary somewhere, too.

Madelyn, nine years old, daughter of Cindy McCormick
Martinusen, author of *Winter Passing*

I think Lucy and Serena are really cool. I can't wait to read the next HIDDEN DIARY book.

Bethany, nine years old, daughter of Janet Holm McHenry,
author of *PrayerWalk* and *Girlfriend Gatherings*

Books by
Sandra Byrd
FROM BETHANY HOUSE PUBLISHERS

Girl Talk
The Inside-Out Beauty Book

THE HIDDEN DIARY
Cross My Heart
Make a Wish
Just Between Friends
Take a Bow
Pass It On
Change of Heart
Take a Chance
One Plus One

THE
HIDDEN
DIARY

Just Between Friends

SANDRA BYRD

BETHANYHOUSE

MINNEAPOLIS, MINNESOTA

Published by Bethany House Publishers
A Ministry of Bethany Fellowship International
11400 Hampshire Avenue South
Bloomington, Minnesota 55438
www.bethanyhouse.com

Printed in the United States of America by
Bethany Press International, Bloomington, Minnesota 55438

Library of Congress Cataloging-in-Publication Data

Byrd, Sandra.
    Just between friends / by Sandra Byrd.
        p.   cm. — (The hidden diary ; bk. 3)
Summary: When Lucy and Serena try to find homes for a lost dog and its
new puppies, Lucy also learns that she doesn't need to do everything herself
and that God wants her to seek help from others.
    ISBN 0-7642-2482-4 (pbk.)
    [1. Christian life—Fiction. 2. Dogs—Fiction. 3. Friendship—Fiction.]
I. Title.
    PZ7.B9898 Ju   2001
    ObFic]—dc21   2001002566

*For Sandy Horton
and Sherri Suminski.*

*A cord of three strands
is not easily broken.*

Contents

Watch Out!

Already late for her beach date with Serena, Lucy rushed into the laundry room attached to the side of their summer cottage and searched for her flower-powers. She'd tossed them in there just last night to be cleaned up a bit. Now the sandals were nowhere to be found. Serena would be there any minute, ready for this week's adventure.

And this week's trouble. Lucy's heart did a little flip at *that* thought.

She threw pieces of dirty laundry over her shoulders— piling up smelly T-shirts to the left, damp towels to the right—till she could see the cool tile floor under the clothes pile. Nothing. She could hardly go barefoot. She hoped her mom would do more laundry soon. It sure did pile up fast.

Then, back in the corner, almost hidden under the dryer, she spied where the still-sandy shoes had landed. *Okay!* She slipped them on and rushed out to the living room.

9

"I'm leaving, Mom." Lucy waved a snappy good-bye to her mother, who was working on a new canvas in the front room. Deep in her work, her mother swirled a paintbrush through the air in a distracted good-bye.

Lucy opened the door to find Serena had just arrived on the front porch, her long black hair twisted up like a Japanese sumo wrestler's.

"Ready?"

"Let's go!" Lucy gave her a thumbs-up. "Want me to carry something?"

Serena shook her head. "If you've got the diary, I've got the umbrella. I've got to be home soon to help my dad, so we need to hurry." She smiled weakly. "I'm kind of . . . well, worried about what the diary might say."

Lucy grinned back. She and Serena had found a hidden diary about two weeks ago. Serena's great-grandmother and *her* best friend, Mary, had written in it long ago, during the summer of 1932. Lucy and Serena had decided that they would spend their summer copying the adventures the diary girls did—week by week. Last night they'd read that the old diary writers had some trouble, which would spell t-r-o-u-b-l-e for Lucy and Serena if they had to copy whatever the 1932 girls did.

The thought brought a smile to her lips. No doubt—this would be an exciting week!

"The usual spot?" Serena asked as they arrived at the beach.

"But of course, madame," Lucy answered, and they claimed a place with the umbrella. Lucy slipped the flower-powers off and let the grains of hot sand spread beneath her feet and squish between her toes.

Serena spent every summer on Catalina Island, twenty-six miles off the coast of Los Angeles. This was Lucy's first summer there. She drank in the steady sun and summer fun like a chilled Dr Pepper, now that her friendship troubles were over—she hoped. Lucy's dad researched rare plants for the university he taught at. This summer they were staying in a university-owned house in the pill-sized town of Avalon on rocky Catalina Island.

Lucy drew the diary out of her beach sack. "Ready for this week's adventure?"

Serena's eyes opened wide. "Ready as I'll ever be."

Lucy cracked open the thin leather diary to the second week's installment and cleared her throat before reading Mary's part. Serena, of course, always read the sections her great-grandmother had written.

"Dear Diary,

We can only jot a tidbit now, as Serena and I are on our way to the community meeting. The town is in an uproar because the community club took a collection for the poor, and some stinker stole the money. A few poor families are eating weeds and breakups, which are the crumbs and broken pieces the bakery has left over!"

As Lucy handed the diary over, something slipped out from between the next two pages. She didn't look at the thing that fell out, but tucked it into her hand, not wanting to disturb Serena's turn to read. "You want to start where your great-grandmother's writing starts?" she asked. Serena's great-grandmother was named Serena, too.

Serena nodded and began to read.

"Some folks are sore, accusing one another of stealing. We're afraid it could tear the town apart. Some are saying people don't want any poor people in town—that they will scare away the tourists and the movie people. But where can they go? The country's in a depression, and each of us has to share what we have. The poor live here, too. Most folks think it's swell to have people to clean houses and serve food—when work can be had, that is."

The handwriting changed again, and as Serena handed the book back to Lucy, she looked at Lucy's hand. "What fell out?"

Lucy opened her hand, and there was a thin paper doll. When she looked at it more closely, she saw it was really *two* paper dolls, cut out of one piece of paper and joined at the hand.

"Cool!" Serena said.

Lucy slipped the paper dolls into her overalls pocket and began reading again.

"We had better scram. More later, after the meeting. Faithful friends, Mary and Serena."

Lucy closed the diary. As they had agreed, they would wait till the end of the week to read the ending.

"Well," she said.

Serena frowned. "I see how their town has trouble, and I'm glad they're helping some poor people. But it's not something we can do."

Lucy's heart sank. She'd been expecting trouble. Big, *exciting* trouble. Not getting-arrested kind of trouble, but amazing-kind-of-adventure trouble. "It's not like people are eating weeds and bread crumbs around here." Lucy looked at the people strolling the sidewalk next to the beach. Most had drippy ice-cream sundaes, scoops and scoops packed into waffle cones. The greasy smell of fish and chips coated the town like a thin layer of sweat. Too little food was definitely *not* a problem as far as Lucy could see.

"So what are we going to do for our Diary Deed?" Serena asked. Each Saturday the two girls read a section of the old diary. They had promised each other they'd do something similar—a Diary Deed—every week by Friday, no matter what trouble or adventure they came across.

"I guess we have to figure out some way we can help people," Lucy grumbled. This did *not* seem like adventure. "We have to think of something fantastic." Lucy squeezed her eyes shut and focused her brain.

"Any ideas yet?" Serena looked out at the channel as the waves bobbed the boats. "You *are* the Queen of Ideas."

Lucy shook her head no.

Serena looked at her watch and took down the umbrella. "I've got to get going or I'll be in trouble."

The two girls shuffled back to the street, dragging the

umbrella behind them. Suddenly, out of the corner of her eye, Lucy spied a fluffy dog hobbling across the road. Its back paw scraped against the street; it wasn't going very fast. Two golf carts came zooming down the street—few cars were allowed on the island, and most people got around in golf carts. The drivers chatted and laughed with one another, not seeming to notice the dog at all.

"They'd better slow down!" Serena said.

Lucy's eyes stayed on the dog. "But they're not. They're going to hit that little dog!"

In one quick movement Lucy dashed into the road to grab the dog and bring it to safety. She scooped the dog into her arms and looked up.

The first golf cart was only feet away—panic flooded the driver's face. "Watch out!" he shouted. Lucy hadn't found trouble. . . . Trouble had found her instead.

I'm not going to make it off the road, Lucy thought in a passing second as she tossed the dog to safety on the grass at the edge of the road. *I'm going to be hit!*

No Pets Allowed

Late Saturday afternoon and evening . . .

Lucy dived for the side of the street and rolled onto the strip of grass next to the sidewalk as she heard the first golf cart's motor choke and die.

A young man jumped out. "Are you okay?"

Lucy looked up into Serena's frightened face and took hold of her outstretched hand. "Yes, I'm fine." She brushed some gravel off of her knee. The red marks on her skin stung.

"Well, you should watch before you cross the street," the man huffed, climbing back into his golf cart.

Mama mia. And you *should watch where you're going instead of nearly running over small dogs,* Lucy thought. She didn't have time to say anything before the man left.

After the carts drove off, Serena asked, "Are you really okay?"

"Yeah," Lucy said. Something fuzzy nuzzled her leg. The little dog rubbed against her leg, making sure she was okay. Lucy reached a hand down to pet it. The dog had fluffy black fur with a white ruff around its neck and little white fur socks.

"Are you sure you should pet a strange dog? It might bite," Serena said.

"Nah, it looks pretty friendly." The little dog licked her hand. Lucy waved the dog away. "Bye, little dog. You'll be safe now. Go home!"

She and Serena headed back toward Lucy's house. Instead of going the other direction, though, the little dog hobbled right alongside Lucy.

"Doesn't it have a home? And why is it limping?" Lucy asked. She leaned over and looked for the dog's tags. "No collar. No tags. Well," she grumped, "what kind of owner would let a dog run around with no tags?"

"Maybe it doesn't have an owner," Serena said.

"Hmm. Well, we can't just leave it here. It might get run over—it's still limping and slow. Let's take it to the animal shelter."

"There isn't an animal shelter on the Island," Serena said.

"Well, the vet, then," Lucy offered.

"The vet only visits from the mainland on Friday," Serena said. "I know because of my cat." The little dog licked Serena's leg before nuzzling up to Lucy's socks again.

"We can't just leave it here! It's hurt!"

"We need to get help," Serena said. "I've got to get going, but I could ask my mom to call her friend Mrs. Marshall. Mrs. Marshall takes care of stray cats, and I know she's helped other animals before."

"Perfect!" Lucy said. "Take it home with you and then give her a call."

"Well . . ." Serena twirled a loose piece of hair before continuing. "I can't. My dad and brother are both allergic to dogs. But if you take her home, I'll have my mom call Mrs. Marshall, and then we can ask her what to do from there."

Lucy stopped walking, and the pooch did, too, standing as still as a stop sign.

I do love dogs, Lucy thought. *But when we moved into this house this summer, the university said no pets allowed. Period.*

They were next door to Lucy's house now, and Stevie, the little neighbor boy, ran from his front porch to the sidewalk. "Did you get a new dog, Lucy?" He abandoned his cars and big yellow dump truck and stumbled toward the dog.

"No, the dog got me." Lucy smiled when she saw the little tail wag at Stevie. "But it's going to Serena's mom's friend's house."

Stevie petted the dog and said, "I always wanted a dog." Then he ran back to his truck.

"I'll call you after we talk with her." Serena snagged the two-way radio that Mrs. Larson made Lucy take with her when she went out without an adult. "I'll take this so I can radio you if your dad's on the Internet."

Lucy nodded.

"I'm sure it will be less than an hour," Serena continued, twisting her watch. "Mrs. Marshall's always home, except in August. I'll ask my mom to call right away, and then my mom and I will come and pick up the dog." Serena started walking backward. "See you later!"

Lucy began to walk around to the side entrance to her house. The little dog stayed with her, wagging its tail and looking up at her with affection. Lucy slowed down so the dog could keep up. Where would the poor thing stay?

No pets allowed.

Well, Lucy wasn't going to be responsible for a little hurt dog getting hit by a car, no matter *what* the university said. She rubbed the soft fur behind the dog's ears, and it licked her hand again, between her thumb and first finger.

Just like Jupiter, Lucy's old dog, used to do.

Lucy had made up her mind. Surely the dog couldn't do any damage to the . . . laundry room!

And anyway, Lucy told herself, *the laundry room isn't really the house. The dog will be gone in less than an hour. What are my choices—let the dog get run over? And I won't tell Mom and Dad. They can't get in trouble with the university if they don't know. I mean, I'd put the dog in the backyard if it were fenced all the way around. But it's my job to keep it safe till Mrs. Marshall tells us what to do.*

Lucy felt wobbly from her belly button to her knees as she opened the door to the laundry room instead of going in the front door. But she opened the door with purpose.

"Come on," she whispered to the dog, who had yet to bark or even whimper. She walked back into the far corner, where her flower-powers had been nestled earlier that afternoon, and made a little bed out of two towels on the floor. She poured some water into an empty coffee cup and set it near the dog. The dog lapped some up, then closed its eyes and snuggled into the towels as if it hadn't rested in a long time.

Lucy hoped her mom wouldn't decide to do laundry right away. Surely she'd let the piles on the floor grow for a few more days.

She closed and locked the laundry room door behind her, then got a glass of water for herself.

Lucy's mom walked into the kitchen. "Pizza tonight! It'll be here in a minute. Did you have a good day?" She tousled Lucy's hair.

"Yes, I did." Lucy didn't want her mom to be so nice to her right now. And she really didn't want her in trouble with the university. It made Lucy's stomach ache. *The dog will be out of here in an hour.*

"Did you pick a new Diary Deed?" Mom asked.

Diary Deed! They had completely forgotten! Now they'd only have *five* days to figure it out and get it done. And the t-r-o-u-b-l-e seemed to have found them anyway. "Not yet," she said.

Mom nodded. "We're going to eat in the living room. I pushed my painting stuff out of the way so we can watch a movie. There's something on that Dad wants to see."

Lucy nodded and then trudged upstairs to her room. She placed the diary on her dresser, near her one sick plant and her one dead plant. She picked the dead one up. Its bone-dry dirt shrank from the sides of the pot, and its leaves crumbled when she touched them, like dried herbs. "Amazing how I can take a perfectly good plant and kill it in less than two weeks without even trying," she muttered, tossing it into the trash can. She opened her Jelly Belly case and searched for something that sounded good. She snapped it shut again, leaving the goodies untouched.

As Lucy set the case back on her dresser, she caught sight of Jupiter's picture.

He was such a cute little dog. So playful. Kind, with loving eyes. Black and white and fluffy. *Like the dog downstairs.* She set the picture down again and bit her lip. Jupiter had died the previous spring.

"I don't know why I always attract the mutts," she said, swallowing a hard lump in her throat. "Mutts get me into trouble."

"Lucy!" her dad shouted from the bottom of the stairs.

Oh no! He found the dog!

She opened the door. "Yes, Dad?" She tried to sound normal, but her tongue felt bitter, almost like it did after throwing up.

"Pizza's here," he said.

Lucy grabbed her mom's two-way radio from her parents' room—in case Serena tried to reach her that way—and headed downstairs.

They watched the movie and ate. The pizza cheese seemed like rubber, the crust like cardboard, the sauce, which Lucy normally loved, tasteless. And it spilled down the front of her shirt. She listened for any noise from the laundry room.

"Are you okay?" her dad asked. "Second thoughts about going to church tomorrow?"

Church! Lucy had almost forgotten. She'd told them that morning that she wanted to try church the next day—

the little church on the green lawn that she'd stopped in a few times before.

She saw the looks on their faces. Her parents had wanted to go to church as a family for a while, ever since they had decided to turn their lives back to Christ.

"No, I still want to go," Lucy said.

Her mom smiled. "Should I iron something for you?"

Lucy's eyes opened wide. "No thanks. I'll just wear something in my closet." The iron was in the laundry room. This was getting worse!

What was she going to do? *Serena!* her mind shouted. *Please, please call!*

The movie dragged on for what seemed like a week, though it was only a couple of hours. Lucy honestly couldn't say what it was about, though her parents laughed all the way through. Lucy couldn't concentrate. She dialed Serena's number once; it was busy, so she went back to the movie.

A bit earlier than usual, her parents announced that they were heading to bed. Lucy's dad checked all the doors, including the one from the house to the laundry room off the side of the house. It was still locked, from when Lucy had locked it earlier.

They went into their room and closed the door. After closing her own bedroom door, Lucy turned on her two-way radio.

"Serena!" she hissed into the mouthpiece. "Are you there?"

Nothing. And now it was too late to call on the phone.

Fear rose in Lucy's throat in an acid mixture. She went

into the bathroom and brushed her teeth. Then she walked back to her bedroom and tried radioing Serena again. She leaned her cheek against the screen of her bedroom window and looked kitty-corner toward Serena's house. The screen would leave tiny waffle prints on her face, but she didn't care.

"Serena!" she whispered into the radio as loudly as she could. This time Serena answered and came to her window, too.

"I'm here," Serena answered. "I saw the light on the radio last time you tried to call me, and turned it on."

"What about Mrs. Marshall?" Lucy cut right to the important part. "What about the dog?"

"My mom called, but Mrs. Marshall wasn't home. We left a message, and I'll try again as soon as we get back from church tomorrow, okay?"

Lucy gulped. "Serena, I have something to tell you."

Silence was thick in the air between the houses. Lucy saw Serena in her window, and they locked eyes.

"The dog is in my laundry room, but my parents don't know. The university said no pets allowed when we moved into this house. That's why when my mom and dad gave me that one hundred dollars for my twelfth birthday last week, they said I'd have to wait till I get home to buy a new dog."

"Oh no," Serena said. "Why didn't you tell me?"

"I don't know. I didn't know what to do. Besides, what was I going to do? Leave the dog outside to get hit?" Lucy practically yelled, her face tight with guilt and accusation. "I'm sorry, I'm just worried."

"Lucy, you can't tell them yet," Serena said. "What if they make you put the little thing out before we talk with Mrs. Marshall?"

Mrs. Marshall would call after church the next day. Lucy didn't want to start going to church with a secret between her and her parents.

The heaviness in her heart spread to her arms and fingers. "I have to tell them," Lucy said. "I know that. What I don't know is what they'll do with the dog!"

"I'm sooo sorry. All I can do is call you in the morning, as soon as I get back," Serena said. She waved to Lucy and clicked off her radio. Lucy sighed and waved back.

She held her breath and opened her bedroom door, tiptoeing the few feet to her mom and dad's bedroom. The door was closed, and no light escaped through the crack at the floor. Dad's snore cranked up, up, up, then dooooooown, like a car motor that couldn't quite start but kept trying every couple of seconds.

What should I do? Lucy stood there, her ticking watch echoing in the dark, narrow hallway. *It's better not to wake a sleeping bear,* she decided, tiptoeing downstairs to let the dog out, then back in. She quietly walked back to her room and set the alarm for 6:23 A.M.

I hope that is earlier than Mom and Dad wake up.

Surprise!

Sunday morning . . . D Day minus five

Through the fog of sleep, Lucy heard the *beep-beep-beep* of her alarm. By the time she rolled over to turn it off, the clock said 6:29.

Why am I getting up so early? All of a sudden, her eyes flew open.

The dog.

She whipped the covers off and leaped out of bed, hoping no one was up yet.

She opened her bedroom door, which led to the hallway, and saw her parents chatting in their room, still in their robes.

Mama mia! They were up already.

The dog would have to go out soon. She'd have to tell them now. She pulled on her own robe and stepped into their room.

"Good morning!" her dad said. "Since when are you an early riser?"

Mom smiled. "Excited to go to *your* church today?" Lucy tried to smile. Ever since Lucy had suggested this little church, her mom had called it "her" church, even though her dad had already checked it out once and liked it.

"Yeah," Lucy said. She wiggled her toes, trying to spend her nervous energy. "But . . . um . . . there's something I need to tell you first."

"Sure," Mom said.

"Would you sit down, please?" Lucy's voice cracked.

Her parents teetered on the edge of their bed. Dad's face tightened.

"Well, don't get mad," Lucy started, "but there's a dog in the laundry room."

Dad stood up. "What? What did you say?"

Lucy took a few steps back. "There's . . . um . . . a dog in the laundry room." She put her hands up in front of her. "But wait! I can explain!"

"I certainly hope so."

Mom said nothing, her eyes and mouth both open wide.

Lucy spilled the words out as fast as she could, explaining about how the little dog was almost run over, how it had no collar, and how it kept following her home.

"Why didn't you ask for help?" Dad bellowed.

Silence sat between them.

"Well . . ." Lucy finally said, "I guess I got used to making my own decisions all last year when neither of you had time to help me."

Her dad sat back down on the bed. He seemed uncomfortable with the reminder of his separation from Lucy's mother last year. After a long minute he said, "I see. I can see how that might have happened. But things have changed—and your mother and I are changing, too."

Lucy's mother nodded. "We're here to help. And we'd like to be in on these things from now on."

Lucy searched their faces. Had they really changed? Had she just not noticed yet?

She waited for the usual accusations to rain down about her impulsiveness. Nothing was said, so she offered, "And I didn't want you to get in trouble with the university."

"Thank you for thinking about us," her mom said. "You act quickly . . ." she began to say.

Here it comes, Lucy thought.

"But with others in mind." Mom smiled.

Lucy let her shoulders and toes relax. "I'm sorry."

"Well." Dad tucked his toes into his slippers. "We had better go down and make sure this little fella is okay. And hasn't 'gone' in the laundry room."

He walked downstairs and through the kitchen and unlocked the door to the laundry room. The little dog wagged its tail. The dirty laundry was no longer in heaping piles; the little dog had dragged each and every piece all over the room, making a crazy-quilt rug across the floor. Lucy thought she saw her dad smile and then try to cover it up.

He bent down and looked at the dog's leg, then carefully examined the pooch all over.

"Get some lunch meat and cheese," he said.

Lucy ran into the kitchen and cut up some ham and string cheese. Then she walked back out into the laundry room. She knelt and set the food in front of the dog, petting its head and rubbing behind its ears. The dog licked her hand.

"Well, Lucy, I certainly hope Serena's mom's friend can help us. Not only am I breaking the agreement I have with the university by having a pet here, but this dog needs more help than we can give her. Unless I'm wrong, she's going to have puppies very soon."

"*PUPPIES?*" Lucy shouted. "Are you sure?"

"I'm pretty sure," her dad said.

"Oh no," Lucy said.

"Oh yes," Dad replied. "I'm going to let her out. I'll meet the two of you in the kitchen in a few minutes, and we'll talk about what to do from here."

Lucy shuffled into the kitchen and looked at the clock. *Not yet seven in the morning. I'm tired already.* Thick, nutty-smelling steam percolated cheerfully through the room.

Lucy sat at the table and let a handful of Cheerios tumble into a Pooh-Bear bowl. "I'm really sorry, Mom," she said.

Mom hugged her. "I know you are."

Lucy pulled back and stared at her mom. Her mom sure hugged her a lot lately, much more than Lucy could ever remember.

"I was going to tell you last night, but Dad was sleeping."

Mom looked at her. "That's not really an excuse," she said quietly. "You had a whole evening last night to tell us."

Lucy looked at her bowl and the dry Cheerios. She didn't speak.

Dad came into the room and poured himself some coffee. "So now what?"

"I guess we hope that Serena's mom's friend calls right away," Lucy answered.

"Yes." Dad looked at her across his mug. "I hope next time something happens, you'll ask for help."

Lucy said nothing.

"Let's get ready for church. We'll find a solution, okay?" Lucy's mother kissed her cheek on the way up the stairs.

No lecture about the problems I've caused? Lucy touched the kiss mark on her cheek. Warmth from it spread from her face to her heart.

Dad nodded. "You, too. Go get ready."

"I'm sorry, Dad."

He finished his coffee. "I know you're sorry, Sparky. We'll hope that the dog is fine while we're gone, and that Serena's mother knows where to take her next."

Lucy stepped upstairs and got dressed.

What if the little dog has her puppies while we're gone? What if the dog needs help and no one is here?

At 10:00 A.M. sharp, the family walked into the little white church on the smooth green lawn. The awkwardness of being at church elbowed the puppy business out of Lucy's mind.

I don't really feel like I belong at any church after being away for so long, she thought. She spied the stained-glass window of Jesus at the front of the church and warmed a bit. *I'm sure I belong to Him, though.*

"Welcome!" The greeter's firm hand swallowed hers as she tried to shake his hand back.

"Thank you," she said. Before she could scan the room to see if anyone she knew was there, her dad whisked them to a center pew.

Lucy sat down and felt her dress twist all around her like the plastic wrapper around a piece of hard candy. She stood up and untwisted, then sat down again.

Well. Here we are.

She reached in front of her and grinned. The pews all had pencils in pockets attached to the seats ahead of them. The pencil in front of Lucy's seat had a smiley face on it and said, *All for One, One for All.*

Lucy snagged the pencil and doodled on the bulletin. She glanced at the people in front of her and to the sides of her. She kind of hoped Jake would be there. He was a friend of Serena's, and now Lucy's friend, too. His family owned Sweet Dreams, an ice-cream and candy shop in town.

Lucy thought he was . . . um, nice.

But he wasn't there this morning. She snuck a peek behind her, too. She didn't see Jake, but even better, she saw Rachel, the teenaged girl she'd met last week when Lucy had come into the church to think and pray.

Rachel waved at her, and Lucy grinned and waved back.

Maybe I do belong at this church!

Claudette and her family were in the back. Just one pew over Lucy spied someone else she had met, Erica. Erica had even come to Lucy's birthday party last week, though she hadn't said much. Lucy caught Erica's eye and waved at her. Erica didn't wave back.

Maybe I don't belong. Lucy sighed.

They sang songs, and Lucy felt better. Music always made her feel better. She let the music fill her, starting from the small place inside her that had warmed when she saw the picture of Jesus. It spread all through her; she felt special toward everyone around her, singing the same songs to God at the same time. It was as though a big net carried them all to Him at once.

They sat down when some announcements were read, and Lucy's dad asked her for the *All for One, One for All* pencil. Lucy handed it over, then watched in horror as her dad wrote on the visitor card, *Interested in the marriage rebuilding classes. Please send information.*

"Dad!" she whispered in his ear. "What are you doing?"

"Getting more information."

Alarms rang in Lucy's head. "But people will know that . . . *you know.* That you and mom have been having some *problems.*" She hissed the last word and then looked around.

Had anyone heard?

"It's okay to ask for help, Lucy," Dad said. Lucy tuned out the pastor and stared at her dad's face, her own heart hardening a bit. Was he trying to say that *he* could ask for help even though *she* didn't?

She searched his face for any know-it-all look, which she had often seen there. Sometimes she felt like he was being the university professor at home, too.

This time she found only peace, softness.

Lucy relaxed and allowed herself to enjoy church, though she didn't look toward Erica's pew again.

As soon as the service was over, Lucy realized with a start: *I haven't thought of the dog for an hour.*

Would the puppies be born when they got home? Was the dog okay?

Needed: A Big Plan

As soon as Lucy got home, before changing her clothes or anything, she ran to the laundry room. Her mom and dad were right behind her.

The fuzzy black-and-white dog looked up at them and gave the smallest of friendly barks.

Lucy looked all around. No puppies. But she noticed the dog had begun to drag other towels over to her little bed.

Her mother sighed. "I know I need to do laundry."

"I'm glad you didn't feel that way yesterday!" Lucy tried to make a joke, but her mother only raised her eyebrows. So much for humor.

Dad stepped into the kitchen and checked the phone. "There's a message here from Serena. Why don't you call her."

Lucy picked up the phone and dialed her friend.

"Hi, how's the dog?" Serena asked.

"She's getting ready to have puppies!" Lucy announced.

"What? Are you kidding?"

"Nope. At least, my dad thinks that's what is going to happen."

Silence.

"Well," Serena said at last. "I didn't tell Mrs. Marshall that, of course, since I didn't know. But she did say we could bring the dog over, and she'd see what was wrong with her foot."

Relief rose from Lucy's heart. "That's great. And . . . um, she'll probably be okay with the puppy thing, too, right? I mean, she does *love* animals."

"I really don't know," Serena said. "But my mom said you can come over in half an hour, and we'll all go over to her house together. Okay?"

"Okay. See ya then." Lucy hung up the phone and quickly told her parents what Serena had said. She popped open a can of Dr Pepper to celebrate and dived into a cold cheese sandwich on soft white bread with mayo.

Shortly after slipping into some cutoffs and a T-shirt, she headed out the front door, snuggling the little dog on her lap in the golf cart as they drove over to meet the Romeros.

Lucy stayed in the cart, but Serena ran over to say hi. Mr. Romero handed each girl a piece of gum from the silver pack in his pocket, and Serena's mother hugged Lucy's mom before each family got into their golf carts and rode off to Mrs. Marshall's house.

They all pulled up in front of a pudding-brown house with iron gates and a trio of ceramic bunnies huddling on the front stoop. Christmas lights still drooped from the eaves, even though it was the middle of summer. Serena knocked on the door. Lucy and the parents followed.

"Hi, honey!" A lady with a tangle of curly red hair opened the door to Serena.

A redhead. Lucy smiled to herself as they stepped inside. *Mrs. Marshall has to be a good person.*

She looked at Lucy. "So this is the dog, eh?" She reached out, and Lucy handed over the little stray.

As soon as Mrs. Marshall took the dog, her eyes opened wide and her voice firmed up. "Did you know that this dog is ready to have puppies?"

"I . . . um, just learned that," Lucy said.

"There's a pound on the mainland. That's it." Mrs. Marshall's breath was a sharp breeze of onions, cheese, and breath mints. Lucy stepped back.

"Well, I don't really want her to go to a pound," Lucy answered. "She might have an owner."

Mrs. Marshall's face softened as she set the dog on the floor. "I don't think she has an owner who cares about her, honey. Maybe someone just got fed up with caring for her. She has no tags. I don't recognize her. And even if she has owners, the puppies won't wait. But I'll help with that."

Lucy heard her mom and dad sigh with relief.

"So you'll help them?" Lucy's dad asked.

Lucy noticed he had said "them" and not "us."

"Yes." Mrs. Marshall popped another breath mint out

of a bright blue tin. "But there's a couple things I got to tell you."

Lucy looked at Serena, who grabbed Lucy's hand.

"First off, I don't have any extra money. I barely got enough for my own dog, Mercedes, and the stray cats around here. You'll have to come up with the money to pay the vet. I'll let her whelp in a play pool I used to keep for my grandson."

"Whelp?" Lucy said.

"Have her puppies. I'll fill it with shredded newspaper so it'll be cozy for them."

"Ah."

"The vet fee will be about one hundred dollars for the mom, probably fifty for each pup, including the shots they'll need in a couple of weeks. If we find the owners by then, maybe they'll pay. But then again, maybe not."

"About how many pups is that?" Serena asked.

"I don't know. Maybe four. Maybe eight."

Eight! That's four hundred dollars. Plus one hundred for the mother dog. Five Hundred Dollars! Lucy's throat closed.

"I'm leaving on July 30. I rent out my house every August. I need these pups and the mother in a good home. If you can't find homes for them, they'll have to go to the pound."

"Oh, I see."

"My suggestion? Find some good homes for the pups this week, just after they're born. Then you can have the new owners cough up the fifty dollars each, and you'll have less money to come up with. And the dog chow is gonna cost someone, too, for a few weeks. I got enough in the back to last till the vet comes this Friday."

Mrs. Marshall stopped and looked at them. "Good enough?" She nodded. "I'll be right back. I'm going to get the pool."

Lucy pulled Serena to a corner of the room. "Where on earth are we going to come up with five hundred dollars by Friday? And homes for puppies that aren't even born?"

"I don't know," Serena said. "Something about Friday . . ." She pursed her lips.

Lucy snapped her fingers. "The Diary Deed! We completely forgot that we have to do something by Friday. An adventure! A challenge!"

"Of course!" Serena said.

"We could make helping the dog and her pups our adventure," Lucy said. "It's not as important as helping real people, of course, like the diary girls did . . ."

"But it *is* helping out," Serena said. "And we could . . . take a collection. Like they did."

"Okay." Lucy started to get excited. "But this is serious. Not just play, you know. And we have to do it with our *own* brain power."

Serena nodded, and they clenched each other's hand for a second.

Lucy walked over to her mom and dad, who had stayed near the door and let Lucy and Serena do all the talking. Serena went to talk with her parents, too.

"We'd like to help out, if we can. I promise I . . . ah . . . won't keep *any* secrets from you. Cross my heart. We think we can do it—do something good to help out, all on our own!"

"It's a big project, Lucy," her dad said. "We can help you with this."

Lucy frowned. *See? He never has any faith in me.*

"We'd like to try on our own, if that's okay. It's our Diary Deed."

"Go ahead and try," her mother said. "But I'd like you to tell me your plans. In advance," she added, chuckling.

Lucy hugged her mother. *Hey! We're getting to be regular huggy twins.* She gave a thumbs-up to Serena. Serena's dad was smiling, and her mom petted the little stray. It looked like Serena's parents said it was okay, too.

Mrs. Marshall came back into the room. "So are we set?"

The girls nodded.

Lucy's dad shook Mrs. Marshall's hand, and Lucy's mother handed Mrs. Marshall a slip of paper with their phone number on it.

"Call us when the pups are born," she said.

Outside, Lucy and Serena leaned on the Romeros' golf cart while Lucy's parents talked a bit with Serena's parents.

"So what should we do?" Serena said. "You're the Queen of Ideas."

"I don't know, but we're going to do it somehow," Lucy said. "We're not giving up and sending them to the pound." She clenched her teeth. *Kids* can *do important things. Kids* can *make a difference. I will think of an idea. I will.*

Lucy looked back at the doorstep, the glass eyes of the

three ceramic bunnies watching them leave.

Five hundred dollars was a lot of money. Friday, when the vet would come and need to be paid, was just five days away.

Sabotage!

The next afternoon, Lucy, Serena, and almost-eight-year-old Claudette sat on the sidewalk in front of Lucy's house. Lucy had promised to baby-sit Claudette for a couple of hours that afternoon. But now she was *so* tired. Lucy had tossed in bed all last night.

"You know," Claudette said, "you kind of look like a dog when you yawn. I can see all of your sharp teeth and everything."

Serena giggled, and Lucy joined in. "Ah . . . thanks, Claudette."

Lucy looked down at Claudette's feet. One brown sock had navy blue diamonds on them; the other was plain brown.

"Claudette," she said. "Your socks don't match again."

"Yes they do." Claudette bit into her apple, then said around a mouthful of fruit, "They both have brown in them."

"We've got to get serious about the dogs," Serena said.

"We've got to think of something—fast."

Lucy sighed. "I know." Where were all her ideas hiding? She had almost nothing to offer to solve this problem. For several minutes the girls sat thinking, Claudette's apple-crunching the only sound.

Finally Claudette set her apple core on the ground. "Maybe you should try to find the dog's owner."

"If there *is* an owner," Lucy said. "I mean, maybe there isn't one."

"Maybe there is," Claudette said. "I think there is one." Lucy resisted the urge to roll her eyes.

"We have to find homes for them. And we haven't figured out how to do a collection without approaching strangers," Serena said.

"How much money do we have ourselves?" Lucy asked. They ran up to her room to see what Lucy had.

"Well, I know that I have thirteen dollars," Serena offered. "Besides what's in savings, and what I have to save to go to Knott's Berry Farm this weekend."

"I'll give all my baby-sitting money. I think I have about twenty dollars, including what Mrs. Kingsley will pay me today." Lucy looked toward her closet, which had built-in drawers. At one time, those drawers hid the key to the old diary; now they hid the one-hundred-dollar bill her parents had given her last week for her birthday. She was saving it to buy her own dog at the end of the summer, when she got back home where there wasn't a no-pets rule. Not that any dog could really replace Jupiter.

"I have six dollars," Claudette said. "I was saving for a new computer program, but I'll give it to the dogs. I wish

I could have one of the dogs. I might get a baby sister later." The Kingsleys were hoping to adopt from China. "But right now a dog would be good."

"The university says no dogs," Lucy reminded her. Claudette's dad worked with Lucy's dad; both families lived in university-owned houses.

Claudette sighed. "I know. I'll still give my six dollars."

Lucy looked at Serena and saw Serena looking toward the closet. Serena knew the hundred dollars was hiding in there, too. But she said nothing.

Lucy softened toward Claudette, who was trying so hard to help. "Maybe you're right about the owner, Claudette," she said. "We could try one thing to find him or her, at least."

Claudette beamed.

"Posters! We can put them up around town," Lucy said.

"Okay," Claudette and Serena said at once. The girls raced downstairs, and Lucy asked her mom if she could have some big rolls of leftover paper from her mom's stash of art supplies. They also asked if it was okay if the posters said to call Lucy's mom for more information. Mom agreed, and the girls took the paper up to Lucy's room.

Lucy took out her Jelly Belly case. "Jelly Bellies, anyone?" She offered beans to everyone. She ate a Cinnamon and a Green Apple together for a candied apple flavor. "Must have been the Christmas lights on Mrs. Marshall's house. They put me in the holiday mood."

Claudette ate the same as Lucy.

Serena giggled and took a handful of Caramel Corn beans. "Must be because I'm corny," she joked.

Claudette cut the papers into squares while Lucy and Serena wrote on them:

Lost Dog!

Pregnant dog, black and white, medium sized.
No collar.
If you know who this dog belongs to,
or would like to adopt a puppy,
please call Mrs. Larson at 3578.

"Okay!" Lucy said. "Now we're getting somewhere. And maybe we'll think of a good way to collect money while we're out putting these around town."

The girls grabbed a roll of masking tape and hung the posters along the street, in a couple of phone booths, and on some street signs. Then they dropped Claudette off at home, and Serena walked back to her own house.

When Lucy arrived home, there was someone waiting for her. Rachel!

"Hi, Rachel!" Lucy said. She tucked her hair behind her ears like Rachel's was.

"Hi, Lucy!" Rachel smiled. "I was working in the church office today and saw a packet of papers that were to be delivered to your mom and dad. I thought I'd deliver them myself."

Horror stomped into Lucy's mind. *Packet of papers? It must be the ones on marriage rebuilding that Dad asked for!* Now *Rachel* knew that Lucy's parents had been working on some problems, too. Suddenly Lucy couldn't breathe too well.

"Oh. Thanks," was all she said.

"I thought I'd see if you wanted to come to the youth

group tonight. It's called Power Hour, and we meet at the church. We play some games, do a devotional, sing, and of course eat snacks. It might be a good way for you to get to meet some people from church. I already asked your parents. They thought it was okay."

"No thanks." It was enough that she'd gone to a church service for the first time in a long time.

Rachel smiled. "Are you a part of a family?"

"Of course!" Lucy stared at her, puzzled. "You met my mom and dad!"

"Well, Christians are a family, too," Rachel said. "The Bible says that two people are better than one, because they can work together. And three are stronger yet. Maybe you should come and meet some other members of your family. New friends."

Lucy looked into Rachel's clear blue eyes. She really meant it. Suddenly Lucy wished she had a big sister like Rachel.

"Maybe I'll come," she finally said. "Can I invite Serena?"

"Sure, invite whomever you want," Rachel said. "I'll be able to walk you home tonight, if your parents can drop you off. I'm going back to the camp later this week. But at least I can introduce you."

"Okay," Lucy said. "Rachel," she added. "Do you want a dog, by any chance?"

Lucy explained about the little lost dog.

"We're a cat family—no dogs allowed," Rachel said. "Sorry!" Rachel headed down the sidewalk. "See you tonight."

"See ya," Lucy said, retucking a loose piece of her strawberry-blond hair. She looked down at her shaggy cutoffs.

I wonder if Mom has done any laundry yet.

Lucy stepped inside the house. Her mom was studying something in one of her art books, but the washing machine hummed in the background. Her dad was on the Internet, home early. A beige envelope was next to Dad's arm. *That must be the church papers,* Lucy guessed. At least it wasn't marked. Maybe Rachel didn't know what was inside, after all.

I hope Mrs. Marshall isn't trying to call and say the puppies are born. Or what if someone is trying to call about the dog while Dad's on the Internet? Maybe someone saw our fliers.

"I'm going to Serena's to see if she wants to come to church tonight," Lucy said.

"I'm starting dinner in a few minutes," Dad answered. "Burgers."

"Mmm," Lucy said. "I'll be back soon." She grabbed both two-way radios, turned them on, and gave one to her mom before stepping outside.

She walked the long way, just to make sure the fliers were secure.

Oh no! When she got to the corner, she saw an empty spot where the flier had been. She raced to the next corner. No flier there, either. Empty pole after empty pole. The fliers weren't on any street sign. She raced to the phone booth. No flier. In fact, she couldn't find any of the fliers. None at all.

Someone had sabotaged their work! But why?

A Call!

Monday evening . . .

Lucy held her side as she ran to Serena's house. After a few quick knocks on the door, Serena answered.

"Hi!" she said. "Come on in."

Lucy stepped into the hallway. "Someone tore down all of our puppy fliers!"

Serena eyes opened wide. "Who would do such a thing?"

Serena's mother stepped into the hallway with them. "Hello, Lucy," she said.

"Hello, Mrs. Romero," Lucy answered. Flour dusted the front of Mrs. Romero's apron; her long brown hair was pulled into a sleek ponytail.

"Bread," she apologized, gesturing at her apron. "Be sure to grab a loaf to take home to your parents before you go."

"Mom, someone tore down all of our fliers," Serena said.

"What fliers?"

"This afternoon we hung some fliers up, telling about the lost dog, and also asking if people wanted any puppies. And now Lucy can't find any of them."

"Oh dear, you can't just hang fliers anywhere in Avalon," Mrs. Romero said. "You need to get permission, a permit. Otherwise the town would be covered in paper."

"A permit? We didn't know."

"I'm sorry, *chiquita*."

"Back to square one," Serena said. "No word from Mrs. Marshall. She called earlier to say that it would be any time now."

The girls walked up the stairs to Serena's room. Her gray kitty was curled up on Serena's bed, as always. She jumped off as Lucy jumped on. "How does your mom know Mrs. Marshall?" Lucy asked.

"She goes to our church," Serena answered.

"*She's* a Christian?" Lucy's voice rose.

Serena giggled. "Yes, why? Is that hard to believe?"

"No, she's just . . . well, you know. A little different." Lucy hadn't figured on Christians being all different looking and acting and all. She smiled. It made her feel better about church.

"It must be the red hair," Serena joked, teasing Lucy about having strawberry-blond hair.

Lucy crossed her legs and cleared her throat. "Speaking of church, I wondered if you might want to come to the youth group at that new church we tried. It's called Power Hour, and this teenaged girl named Rachel came to invite me today."

"I know Rachel!" Serena said.

"You do?" Lucy asked.

"Sure. This island is pretty small. She's really cool."

"So you'll come, then?" Lucy's hopes climbed.

"Um . . . no."

"No?"

"Don't be offended. But I have my own church and youth group, so I think I'll just stick with that," Serena said. "We're still Faithful Friends, of course. As always."

Lucy closed her eyes for a minute. Weird. They did everything together. And Serena's faith was one of the reasons Lucy was so drawn back to the Lord. Should she go to Serena's church instead?

Neither of them said anything in the silence.

No. Lucy had liked the little church, and it was the one her mom and dad wanted to attend, too. And of course, Christians were all brothers and sisters anyway, no matter where they went to church. "I think I'll go to Power Hour anyway."

"Good!" Serena said. "Want me to paint your nails for the occasion?"

"Yes, indeed!" Lucy held her hands out as Serena shook a bottle of pearly purple polish.

"What are you wearing? Will purple match?"

"I'm wearing whatever is clean." Lucy laughed. "But I'm hoping my jeans and violet pullover are clean, so purple would be great."

After Serena finished, Lucy said, "I'd better get going. My dad was starting some burgers." Lucy cleared her throat. "Would it be okay if I prayed for us and for the dog?"

Last week when Serena had slept over, she'd prayed out loud for the two of them. This time, Lucy felt she wanted to.

Serena smiled. "Sure. But I've been meaning to tell you something, and I want to do it before we pray. I'm sorry I told you not to tell your parents the other night. I was afraid for the dog, but it was the wrong thing to say. Will you forgive me?"

"Of course!"

Serena's face grew cloudy. "I don't want the puppies to go to the pound. And so far, we only have thirty-nine dollars."

Lucy's heart dropped. "I know." They'd never make it.

"I don't think we're going to find the puppies homes by Friday, in time to get the money," Serena said.

Lucy agreed. They were in over their heads this time.

They sat cross-legged across from each other on the smooth wood floor. A faint citrus memory of the lemon oil used to clean them rose from the warm boards. Each girl closed her eyes.

Lucy started, "Dear God. I know it's not the same as the diary girls helping people, but I wonder if you would help us to help this dog and her puppies. She needs some help, and we want to help her. But we're not sure what to do. Could you please tell us what to do? The dog kind of looks like Jupiter. I'd really like to help her. Thank you. Amen."

As she prayed, Lucy felt special warmth between her

and Serena, like a candle that burned brighter. When they prayed together, something strong happened.

But now she had to get back home. She grabbed a loaf of bread on her way out.

and gulping down a burger and a small haystack of fries, Lucy and her mother walked to Power Hour. Lucy kept her two-way radio with her and promised she wouldn't go anywhere except home afterward, when Rachel would walk with her.

Lucy walked into the room in the church's downstairs, where clumps of kids sat talking and munching chips. The room was small but bright with new carpeting and cool beach weavings on the wall. Lucy took a chair in the back of the room and sat there alone.

I feel like a complete cornball. She looked around for Rachel and saw that she was talking to someone else.

Well, I can't sit here like a dead plant. She walked over and started a conversation with some others, who were kind and welcoming. It put a little breeze in her heart.

After a bit Rachel caught Lucy's eye and brought some of the other leaders over to meet her, including the couple who ran the youth group. The lady had thick, groovy eyeglass frames.

I wish I wore glasses, Lucy thought. *Cool glasses.*

After a few minutes Lucy and Rachel grabbed a drink. No Dr Pepper. They obviously needed some help in the refreshments department.

Just then Erica walked into the room. She had brought her best friend, Amy. They'd come to Lucy's birthday party last week.

"Lucy!" Amy shrieked. Her little gold round earrings matched her softly rounded face. She ran over and gave Lucy a warm hug. Lucy's heart opened.

"Look, Erica, Lucy is here."

"Hi," Erica said. She tucked her hands into her sweat-jacket pocket, but not before Lucy saw how broken out they were with a skin rash. Erica didn't look too happy to see Lucy. "Did you bring Serena?"

"No," Lucy said.

"Are you still friends?" Erica demanded.

"Of course!" Lucy felt her heart clamp back shut like a clamshell.

Amy pulled Lucy over to sit by them.

During the Power Hour everyone introduced themselves. Lucy was a bit disappointed that Jake wasn't there, since he was just a little older than she was and went to this church. But a lot of people talked to her after the skit and the devotion. By the time they all sat together in a circle for prayer time, she felt connected to them somehow. It was like they were each some of Claudette's Legos that had been snapped together for this time. Even though they'd unsnap and go home soon, they'd still be a set somehow.

So when Rachel asked if there was anything anyone wanted prayer for, Lucy snuck her hand halfway up.

"Lucy?"

"Well," Lucy said, "my friend Serena and I found this lost dog, and the dog's going to have puppies soon!"

A chorus of "oohs" and "ahhs" rose from the circle.

"We need to find homes for the puppies this week, and also raise some money to pay for the vet visit." Lucy quickly explained about Mrs. Marshall, then ended with, "I'd really like it if you guys would pray for us, because we don't see how we can make it all work."

During the circle time, several people prayed for the puppies, but also for Lucy, and thanked God that she was there.

Lucy squeezed her eyes shut tight. Why would she feel like crying when people were praying for her?

When she felt it was safe, she opened them again.

Amy and Erica walked over to talk to someone else, and as Lucy looked for Rachel, a boy came over.

"Hi," he said. "My name's Roger. I wanted to talk to you about the dogs."

His bangs were so long Lucy couldn't see his eyes. But when he brushed them away, he looked very kind.

"Hi," Lucy said.

"I . . . uh . . . I've been thinking about getting a dog. If you'll give me your phone number, I'll call you after I talk with my parents."

"Sure!" Lucy said. She scribbled her number—and her mother's name—on a piece of paper. "Have your mom call my mom. And thanks!"

Roger smiled and went back with his friends. A little thrill ran up Lucy's spine.

One puppy might have a home! It was only a little spark, but it fed her hope.

Rachel was waiting by the door, and Lucy didn't want

to make her late. She headed in her direction.

As she did, Erica came up and grabbed Lucy's arm. "I just got an idea," she said.

"Oh?" Lucy said. She looked over at Rachel, who was holding her purse and everything. Lucy didn't want to make her late!

"Well," Erica said, "you could put up a sign in front of the dog lady's house about the puppies. That way, if anyone wanted one, they would know where to go."

How many people would walk by a house and want a puppy? Lucy's doubt must have shown, because Erica frowned.

"It's a dumb idea, I know," Erica mumbled. "Sorry to bother you." She turned away.

"Wait!" Lucy said. "It's not that!" But Erica hurried toward the other half of the room.

"Lucy?" Rachel called. "We'd better go."

Lucy grabbed the notebook the leaders had given her and left. Erica's back was toward Lucy.

Well, if she's going to walk away before I can explain, there's nothing I can do, Lucy thought. But she felt sad and cold and definitely unsnapped from Erica and Amy as she walked home beneath the nodding stars.

Rachel dropped her off, and Lucy thanked her. She squeaked open the front gate and opened the door.

As soon as she stepped into the cottage, her dad called out, "Lucy! Telephone! It's Mrs. Marshall about the puppies!"

Dialing for Doggies

Tuesday . . . D Day minus three

The next day Lucy sat in the windowless alcove off of the living room playing the piano. Ever since the night before, when she'd gotten the call that the puppies had been born, she'd been dying to go and see them. Now Serena was on her way over to do just that.

Lucy closed her eyes and let her hands wander over the keyboard, searching out familiar keys and playing them by feel. She pounded out one of her favorite Beach Boys tunes and lost herself jamming with the notes.

"Hi."

At the sound of Serena's voice, Lucy immediately took her hands off the keys, as if they burned her fingertips, and slammed the piano cover down.

"Why did you stop playing?" Serena asked. "That was great. I love that song."

"Yep. Well, let's go," Lucy said.

"No, really, please finish the song," Serena said.

Lucy said nothing. Then she swiveled around on the piano bench. "Do you remember the first week we were friends, and you asked me if there was anything I was afraid of?"

Serena sat down next to her. "Yeah . . ."

"Well, there are three things I can think of that I'd rather die than do. Playing the piano in front of other people is one of them. I never do recitals. I did one once and forgot every single note. I forgot how to read music. I had to walk off the stage in the middle of the song. I waited for my parents outside the concert hall and haven't done one since."

Serena slowly nodded. "This isn't a recital, though."

Lucy's eyes stared into Serena's. "I just can't." She stood up. "Is it okay if we take Claudette? I told her we'd bring her by when we went to see the puppies. She doesn't have to stay the whole day, though."

"Sure." Serena checked her watch. "Mrs. Marshall called before I left and said not to come for another hour. Wanna sit outside?"

"Okay." The two girls sat on Lucy's porch swing, letting the salty breeze cool their skin. The swing creaked and groaned with every sway, competing with the sound of boat horns honking in the harbor.

"I have some really good news," Serena said. "I could hardly wait to tell you."

"Great!" Lucy said. "Let's have it!"

"Well, I was thinking of how we could collect money. What if we made a collection can, and then I drew a picture of the dog and wrote the information on it, and we hung it under the can? We could ask Jake if we could put the can at Sweet Dreams. Maybe we could get lots of donations from the tourists that come in this week. And it will be fun to put *all* the money in one place and see it grow into a huge amount!"

It really *was* a great idea. Lucy wished it had been hers.

"Does that sound too weird to you?" Serena asked.

Lucy worked hard to pep her voice up. "No, not at all. In fact, I think it's a great idea."

Serena searched her face. "You don't look too happy."

Lucy looked down at her knees. "Well, to be honest, I feel bad that I usually have some good ideas and this time zippo! The only idea I had was the fliers, and look what happened to that. Nothing. You thought of Mrs. Marshall, and you thought about the collection can."

Serena took her hand. "You know what? I got this idea after you prayed for us last night."

Lucy looked up from her knees into Serena's face. Then she smiled. Maybe things worked differently in God's world than the way she thought they should.

"Let's get a collection can!" Lucy jumped off of the swing and raced into the house. Serena followed.

"Mom! Serena has a great idea!" She tumbled into the laundry room, where her mom was finishing up the last load, and told her about the collection can.

"Wonderful!" her mom said. "And I'll let Serena have a piece of my good art paper to draw a picture on." She led them into the living room, where her art supplies were.

Soon Mrs. Larson and Serena were leaning together over a blank piece of paper, a couple of soft-lead pencils in hand. Lucy dashed into the kitchen.

Dad's mombo-sized coffee can! It's perfect. Now, what to put the grounds in?

Lucy peered into the almost-full can, staring at the dark brown grounds. She dug through the cupboards, looking for a Tupperware container, but there wasn't much in the university's kitchen. Finally she pulled out ten little sandwich bags and dumped the coffee into them. The counter looked as if she'd been potting plants in Folgers, but she didn't care. The can was perfect.

She cut a slit in the lid, then grabbed some leftover white shelf liner from under the sink. After cutting a large, wide strip, she wrapped the self-sticking paper around the can and cut it to size. Now the can was ready for gobs of money! Lucy returned to the living room, where Serena was just finishing the dog drawing.

Serena attached the picture and paper with the information on it with a piece of Mrs. Larson's canvas tape.

"High five, girl friend," Lucy said. She held up her hand, and Serena slapped it in return.

"Let's stop at Sweet Dreams on the way to Claudette's," Serena suggested.

Lucy's heart did a little flip. "Do I look okay?" She tucked her hair behind her ears and straightened her shorts.

Serena grinned. "Any reason in particular that you care to look nice for *that* shop?"

Lucy playfully punched Serena on the arm, and they headed to the ice-cream shop.

In only a few minutes they were there. Jake stood on a

stepladder in front, painting a waffle-cone sundae on the outside window of the shop.

Does everyone have to be an artist? Lucy giggled to herself.

The pink-and-white-striped shop was on the corner of one of the busiest streets in town. Tourists walked passed them as Serena explained to Jake about the canister and the little dog.

"I can ask my mom what she thinks," Jake offered. They followed him into the shop. His mom was behind the counter, weighing some fudge for a customer. Her hair was pulled back in a loose bun with a soft pretty net over it.

"Mom, this is Lucy, Serena's friend."

"Hello, Lucy."

"Hello," Lucy said politely.

Jake explained about the dog, and his mother nodded. "We could keep the container on the front counter, near the cash register, so people can donate till Friday," she said. "Stop back on Thursday to see how it's going."

"Thank you," Serena said.

"You're welcome," she said.

"Yeah, you're welcome," Jake said, turning his cap to face forward and pulling down the tip of it in Lucy's direction.

The girls took off up the street. They stopped at Claudette's house.

Lucy grinned when Claudette came out of her house. Today Claudette had on striped toe socks that reached her knees, and flip-flops.

"I'm ready!" Claudette announced.

"Let's go!" The three girls walked as fast as they could to Mrs. Marshall's house.

Lucy knew that past the iron gates, the tired Christmas lights, and the glass-eyed bunnies were the puppies. Mrs. Marshall opened the door and let them in.

They walked in front of the pool and knelt down. Lucy had expected to like the pups. But instead of turning soft, her heart completely melted.

The mother dog lay on her side, and she licked Lucy's hand when she reached into the pool. The puppies looked like five little fuzz balls. Their eyes were still closed, and they nuzzled close to their mother. Four of the puppies scrunched in. The fifth puppy, a black one with a milk splash of white fur on its head, rolled backward when the others nudged her out of being fed.

Lucy giggled, and the other girls did, too. "Forward, fuzzy one, forward," she said. Mrs. Marshall said it would be okay if they gently touched the puppies, and Lucy picked up the topsy-turvy backward roller and put it closer to the mother so it could eat, too. Mrs. Marshall told Lucy that one was a girl.

Lucy's heart reached out to the puppy. "I'll work really hard to find you a home," she whispered to the pup. She rolled backward again, and Lucy laughed.

Maybe I could have a puppy . . . one of these puppies.

If someone could just keep the puppy for a few weeks from the time Mrs. Marshall left in August till Lucy went back home, she could do it. But who? Lucy ran through the possibilities in her mind. Not Claudette, since she lived in university housing, too. Not Serena, because of the allergy problem. She didn't know Jake well enough to ask him—too embarrassing! Rachel had already said they were cat people.

Lucy's shoulders sagged.

The girls left the pups to the mother dog, promising to come back and visit soon.

Serena looked at Lucy. "We have to find them good homes."

Lucy nodded. "For sure!" She turned to Mrs. Marshall. "How can we help them find homes?"

"Call everyone you know," Mrs. Marshall said. "I'd help, but I've already placed pets with everyone I know."

The girls dropped Claudette off at her house, then ran back to Serena's. They raced up to her room and got out her butterfly address book.

"Let's call all of the girls. Since Roger might want one, we only have to find homes for four more! With all the girls I know, surely *one* might want a dog."

Serena dialed the first number. The answer was no. She dialed again, and the answer was no. She called almost everyone she knew, except for Amy and Erica, since they'd been at Power Hour and already knew about the dog.

Lucy called Betsy and Jenny. Both already had pets. She even muscled up enough courage to call Julie, who was not exactly her biggest fan. Julie flat-out said, "No."

The two girls dropped to the floor. They'd called all their friends. And the fluffy pups still did not have homes waiting for them.

Neither girl mentioned the pound.

8

In the Attic Drawer

Lucy's parents walked Lucy to Claudette's house to spend the evening while they went to their marriage class at church. Lucy waited for Mr. and Mrs. Kingsley to say something about where her parents had gone. They obviously knew that her parents had separated last year, since Claudette's dad worked with Lucy's dad and had talked with him about the Lord during the separation. They didn't say anything to Lucy tonight, though. They just ate dinner together and joked and did a craft with Claudette and her.

A couple hours later, Lucy's parents came to pick her up. No one spoke on the way home, instead enjoying the breeze and the *whoop-whoop-wooo* night bird calls in their nesting trees. Lucy noticed her parents held hands.

When they got home, Lucy's mom set a bunch of papers on the counter.

Lucy stuck her nose near the counter like a little dog and looked them over. "Can I read any of these?"

"You can read the brochure," her mom said. "The rest is personal." Lucy picked up the one her mom handed her.

"I have good news for you," her mom continued. "There was a couple in our class, and they said their son is interested in a dog. His name is Roger. I guess he met you last night at Power Hour."

"Will they take one for sure?" Lucy said, pulling her nose from behind the brochure so she could look at her mom.

"For sure."

"Yes! What were *his* parents doing there?"

Her mother smiled and stuck some microwave popcorn in. "The same thing we were. Getting help and giving help to one another."

Lucy closed the brochure. "Oh. I guess so." On the front of the brochure she read, *"You are members of God's very own family . . . and you belong in God's household with every other Christian." Ephesians 2:19.*

A family. Isn't that what Rachel said? My family.

Lucy's mom came and sat down on a breakfast stool next to her. The microwave popcorn reminded Lucy of the Fourth of July.

"So it's kind of like the people at church—and all other Christians, really—are a family?" Lucy asked.

"Exactly!" Mom said. "Even if you don't know them all too well."

The microwave beeped, and Mom tore open the seam

of the bag and shook the steamy, soft nuggets into three bowls.

"I'm going to paint for a while before I forget what it was I wanted to touch up." Lucy's mother grabbed two of the bowls, delivered one to Lucy's dad, who was on the computer, and went into the living room.

Lucy tucked her bowl under her arm, grabbed her book from the counter, and walked upstairs.

A family.

She got into her room and shut the door. Then she peeked out the back of her window. She could see Serena's shadow through her curtain, leaning over her desk. The sight warmed her. Serena was like a sister to her already. The twin sister she'd always wanted and never had. A sister who'd taught her some things about God. Like about praying.

Lucy sat down on her bed and folded her hands in her lap.

"God, I'm not too good at this praying thing yet. I don't have a lot of practice. I feel like when I first started riding my bike and things were kind of wobbly and I wasn't sure if I was doing it right. I mean, am I supposed to pray again for the same thing that I already prayed for? The dog and the puppies, I mean, of course. Thanks for Roger, but there are four more puppies."

She stopped for a second, and then whispered what was heaviest on her heart.

"Please find a home for that little roly-poly one with the white spot on her head. Amen."

As soon as Lucy finished praying, she thought about Erica.

I guess Erica is family, too, then. She remembered Erica huffing away after they talked last night at church.

Maybe Erica is the strange member of the family. Lucy smiled. *Every family has one.*

Then she remembered her own thought, about how Erica's idea wouldn't work. Her face screwed up.

Hey, maybe I'm the strange member of the family, not Erica. Lucy reached for the telephone and the list of names Serena had written out last week for her birthday. She found Erica's name on the list and, after glancing at the clock to make sure it wasn't too late, dialed.

"Hello?"

"Hello, this is Lucy Larson. May I please speak with Erica?"

"Yes."

"Hello?" a small voice answered.

"Erica? This is Lucy. You had a great idea, and I was wondering if it would be okay if we do your poster idea for the puppies. Maybe people really will see the sign as they walk by Mrs. Marshall's house."

"Do you mean that?" The voice was medium sized now.

"I really do," Lucy said. "I'd like you to help. Maybe you and Amy could come over to my house tomorrow and make the poster with Serena and me. If you want to, that is. We could do it all together, with everybody's help."

"I'd like that! And I'll bet Amy would, too. Lemme ask

my mom." The phone clattered on the counter, and in a minute or two she was back.

"I can come. I'll call Amy, too, and then I'll call you in the morning to see what time we can come over."

"Whoops! Can you hold on a minute?"

Lucy ran down the stairs.

"Mom? Can I invite a couple of girls to come over tomorrow and make a poster to put at Mrs. Marshall's house?"

Her mom set down her brush for a moment, and with a twinkle in her eye, she said, "Sure, Lucy. And thank you for asking first."

Lucy grinned back and took the stairs up two at a time.

"Okay, it's all set. Talk with you in the morning."

"Okay! Bye." Erica's voice was strong and happy at the end.

Lucy set the portable phone on her dresser. The paper dolls from the old diary still lay there.

I better remember to put those back soon, or they might get ripped.

She lifted up her picture of Jupiter and stared through the glass. Jupiter had a Santa hat on; they'd taken the picture last Christmas. Lucy remembered how he'd been afraid of the plastic Christmas moose that sang "Grandma Got Run Over by a Reindeer."

In spite of herself, Lucy giggled at the memory. *Good old Jupiter.* Seconds after giggling, her eyes filled with tears. She sighed. *Good old Jupiter.*

If it were Jupiter, she'd want to spend every bit of energy she had finding a good home for him. She glanced at her closet, where the attic drawers held her treasures. Jewelry. Money.

Lucy walked over to the drawer with her birthday money in it and took out the hundred-dollar bill. She unfolded it and looked over both sides.

If she gave it, she wouldn't have enough money to buy her own dog at the end of the summer, and she might not have that much money again for a long time. But if she kept it, they might not have enough to pay for food and care for the mother dog and the puppies.

Escape!

Wednesday morning . . . D Day minus two

"I'll do the dishes." The next morning Lucy scooped the breakfast plates off of the table and gave them a quick rinse before stuffing them into the dishwasher. "Where's the broom?"

Her mother raised her eyebrows. "Is the queen coming for tea?"

Lucy giggled. "No, I just want it to be nice when the girls get here. And can we use some of your art board for the poster?"

Mom scrunched up her face. "I don't know. It's expensive."

"Please?" Lucy clasped her hands together in the begging position.

"All right."

"And some paint and brushes, too? Please?"

"Lucy, that stuff costs money. I earn my living painting, you know."

Lucy sank to her knees on the ground, keeping her hands closed in the begging position. "It's for a good cause."

Her mother tousled her hair. "All right. Don't make a mess." Then she left for the living room.

Lucy scraped some dried poached-egg goo off of the table with her fingernail, and then wiped it into a paper towel. It had stained the underside of her fingernail yellow, but who cared? The table was ready for the girls to get to work.

Lucy sprayed some citrus air freshener in the room to hide the egg smell and sniffed the air. Still stinky. She sprayed some more orange-blossom scent into the air, waving the can throughout the room while she counted to twenty.

Five minutes later, the doorbell chimed.

"Come on in." Lucy scooted Serena into the kitchen. "Help me get the paints and brushes out."

The two girls ran into the living room. Lucy's mother concentrated on her own work and didn't seem to notice them. Lucy grabbed some watercolor trays and four sticky brushes out of a baby food jar. Serena grabbed some firm art board. Then they headed to the kitchen.

Serena scooted her chair closer to Lucy's. "Did you guys have oranges for breakfast?" she asked. "It smells so orangey in here."

Lucy felt her face color as she shook her head.

"My mom said we can put a poster up on personal property, even though we can't on public property, so our poster will be safe. And she checked with Mrs. Marshall to make sure it's okay with her."

Lucy smiled in relief, and then the doorbell rang. When they opened it, Erica and Amy stood there.

"Ready for work?" Serena asked as they hugged one another. Erica even gave Lucy a stiff hug.

"Ready!" Amy said. "Do you think this will really help?"

Erica's face opened up for a minute.

"Yes, I do," Lucy said. "It's a great idea. I wish I'd had it."

Erica beamed, and Lucy smiled back.

Each girl took a brush. Serena sketched out what they should write, and the other girls painted in the letters. A spot of brown flew onto Lucy's face.

"Ooh, a beauty spot," Amy said, giggling.

"I can use all the help I can get." Lucy dipped her brush into the brown and dotted another one near her eye. "Better?"

"Even more beautiful," Serena said. "How about one for me?"

Lucy dotted two beauty marks on each of them: one near the eye, and one near the mouth.

"Aren't we lovely?" Amy giggled. The four of them laughed out loud after Lucy toted a mirror in from the hallway.

"I don't think they're cute. They look like moles!" Erica said. The four of them burst out again.

As soon as the poster dried, Serena offered to call Mrs.

Marshall. "I'll see if she's ready for us to come over and put up the poster."

"And I brought some money for your collection," Amy said. "Can we stop by and put it in the can?"

Lucy had mentioned to Erica about the collection can at Sweet Dreams. "Of course. We're hoping to get a big stash of money in there."

"I brought some, too," Erica said.

"Thanks," Lucy said. She ran upstairs to get her birthday money, as Serena called it. She slipped the one-hundred-dollar bill out of the drawer and jammed it deep into her pocket. Then she grabbed her large Jelly Belly container and put it into her woven shoulder bag. She ran downstairs.

"Mrs. Marshall says we can come in half an hour. If we roll up the poster, we can stop at Sweet Dreams and then head to her house," Serena said. "She's not going to be there, but she said the puppies and the dog are in the front yard."

The girls nodded, and after rolling up the poster, they headed to Sweet Dreams.

Jake wasn't there, but his mother welcomed them into the shop. "Haven't checked the donations," she said, "but quite a few people put in money."

"Great!" Lucy said. First Erica put her money into the can, then Amy. After they were done and had moved away, Lucy secretly slipped her hundred-dollar bill into the can. A mix of sorrow, contentment, concern, and peace swept through her.

The girls left the store and walked up the street toward

Mrs. Marshall's house. They put the poster on the fence with some masking tape. Erica had drawn a five-four-three-two-one-zero countdown on the board. Each time a puppy was spoken for, Mrs. Marshall would cross off one number so they'd know how close they were to their goal. They'd already painted through the five, since Roger had spoken for one of the pups.

They opened the gate and went to the shady part of the yard. Mrs. Marshall had left the pool under a tree, and the mother dog rested while the pups nestled nearby. Roly-poly milk-splash was on the outside. Lucy reached her hand in and gently parted two of the pups and scooted her favorite in, too.

Serena watched her. "You like that one the best, don't you?"

Lucy nodded. "I want her to have a home. Even if . . ." She didn't finish the sentence.

Serena nodded and placed her hand on Lucy's arm. "I know."

Just then they heard a commotion.

"OH NO!" Erica's voice rang out.

Lucy and Serena turned around just in time to see Mercedes, Mrs. Marshall's dog, run out of the unlatched gate.

10

Don't Give Up

Wednesday afternoon and evening . . .

The girls chased the dog down the street, but Mercedes was much faster than they were. Amy remembered to close the gate so at least the other dog couldn't get out, too, while Serena, Erica, and Lucy sped off.

Lucy's heart was an ice cube that dripped liquid cold throughout her blood. What if a car hit Mercedes? What if she took off somewhere the girls couldn't follow? What would Mrs. Marshall say if she came home right now?

The girls stopped running when Mercedes stopped at the top of the road.

"We can't outrun her," Amy said. "My dog can always outrun me."

"What can we do, then?" Serena asked.

The girls stood there and thought.

"We can try to tempt her back with a treat," Amy said.

"That just might work," Erica agreed. "Good idea!"

Serena went back into Mrs. Marshall's yard to see if

there were any treats around while the other three girls kept an eye on Mercedes, who was still sniffing bushes up the road. In a minute Serena returned with a smoked pig's ear. She held it out by her fingertips.

"Gross. It really looks like an ear. But the bag said, 'Dogs Love 'Em,' so I guess it will do."

The girls crept toward Mercedes, holding the pig's ear out like a carrot on a stick. Soon Mercedes pranced down the road and snatched the pig's ear from Serena's outstretched hand.

Amy scooped the dog up, and they ran back into Mrs. Marshall's yard, where they set the dog down and then left—closing the gate firmly behind them.

Once out on the street, they sat on the curb underneath their poster and giggled.

"Can you imagine if Mrs. Marshall had come home?" Amy asked.

"*Big* trouble," Serena said. "After all she's done for us. Trouble."

Lucy linked arms with Serena on one side and Erica on the other. Erica linked arms with Amy, who was next to her.

"So what's a little trouble when it's just between friends?" Lucy asked. The four of them giggled.

All of a sudden Erica stopped laughing. "Oh no!" she said.

The others got serious quickly. "What is it?" Amy asked.

Erica touched Amy's face in two places. "The moles! I mean, beauty marks! We've been walking all over town with these on, including in Sweet Dreams!"

The girls laughed again, so hard that some people driving by in their golf carts stared as they passed by.

Lucy didn't care. She looked up at the poster and thought again about the canister at Sweet Dreams, remembering what Rachel had said about two being better than one and three being stronger still. Lucy, Serena, Amy, and Erica. Four might be better yet! She just knew Erica's poster plan was going to work.

Then Lucy had another thought. Maybe Erica could keep the puppy for her for a few weeks—if Lucy could get one, that is. She pulled Erica aside.

"If I ask for one of these puppies, do you think you could maybe keep it at your house for a few weeks at the end of the summer, just till I go back home?" Lucy explained about the university's no-pets policy.

Erica wouldn't look her in the eye. "Maybe," she said. "I'll let you know."

Maybe! Lucy thought. *Not no—maybe!* She guessed that Erica would have to ask her parents, of course. *Ask them soon!*

The girls grabbed a hot dog together in town, then left to go to their own homes. Lucy opened her front door but saw no one. She slipped her flower-powers off and headed toward the stairs. As she did, she heard her parents' voices behind closed doors upstairs. They normally didn't close their bedroom door during the day, unless there was a problem.

Lucy gulped, remembering how they used to go into their room and close the door when they were fighting and didn't want her to hear. Maybe the marriage class last night had *not* been helpful—but harmful!

She walked quietly up the stairs. She wasn't exactly eavesdropping, but she did walk very slowly past their room.

"Well, then I guess that's what we'll have to do," her dad said. "Two hundred dollars toward the dog seems like a lot, but there doesn't seem to be another choice."

She heard her dad's key jingle in his pocket as he stood up. Lucy skedaddled down the hall and into her room. She plopped down on her bed.

See? He doesn't *believe we can do it on our own*, Lucy fumed. *He's going to do it his way after all.* Which was not at *all* what the Diary Deed was supposed to be about. She just *knew* they could do it by Friday, when they had to pay the vet—and Lucy and Serena would write in their own friendship diary.

Lucy stood up, ready to march down the hall and tell her dad she didn't need his money if he couldn't have faith in her and her friends.

As she did, she noticed she'd left the drawer open in her attic closet. Drawn to it, she stepped inside the closet and looked inside the empty drawer. Her one-hundred-dollar bill used to be there, and now, of course, it wasn't.

Did you *have a lack of faith in your collection canister and your plan when you donated* your *money?* a voice inside her head and heart spoke to her. *Or were you just being kind to the dog, wanting the best for it? Wanting to help.*

Lucy slowly closed the door. Of course. She just wanted

to help. And maybe her dad did, too. Isn't that what families were all about, anyway?

She felt bad that she'd had snippy thoughts when her dad first asked if they could help back at Mrs. Marshall's house on Sunday.

Lucy set her two-way radio on the dresser, and as she did, she noticed the paper dolls again, the ones they'd found in the old diary. She lifted them up carefully. They still held hands, unbroken after all these years. She slipped them back into the old diary.

With nothing else to do, Lucy pulled her scissors out of her top desk drawer and reached for the roll of leftover paper from the collection-can sign. First she folded the paper over and over. Then she snipped and sheared and cropped. When she'd started, she'd meant to only make two dolls so that she and Serena could put them in their own diary. But cutting was so fun, she had a better idea. She cut sets of the dolls—some five dolls together, some three dolls together—and stacked them. Then she got out her markers and colored the dolls. When she was done, she put the dolls into envelopes. Finally she tucked them into her drawer, where they would rest until just the right moment. As soon as the drawer was shut, her dad knocked on her door.

"Chinese food tonight—remember?" He smiled. Lucy smiled back at him. She wanted to tell him she was sorry for thinking such bad things about him, but if she did, he'd know she'd overheard his conversation about donating to the dog fund. Instead, she got up and gave him a hug.

"What's that for?" he asked.

"Just for being my dad," she answered. "And for everything you've done—and for giving to the dogs."

Her dad looked at her strangely. "I haven't even made a donation yet." He looked at Lucy. "But we can stop on the way to the restaurant and I'll do just that. Okay?"

Lucy nodded, not wanting to butt in on his secret. She understood. He didn't want her to know how much he was giving. "Okay."

The three of them strolled downtown to Sweet Dreams.

Good thing I took the time to wash off those goofy beauty marks, Lucy thought as they stepped into the shop. Jake wasn't there, nor his mom. Instead, someone Lucy had never met worked behind the counter.

Her dad nodded hello, then slid a few crisply folded bills into the canister. They left and walked a few doors down to the restaurant.

The gold and red lanterns swayed back and forth in the Avalon breeze like lithe Chinese dancers. The door chimes jingled as they entered.

After a dinner of sweet-and-sour pork, tender rice, and lemon chicken, Lucy's dad paid the bill.

They grabbed a couple of cookies on the way out.

"Did you see what that sign called the cookies?" her mother asked, cracking hers in half like an egg.

"Nope. What?"

"Thoughtful cookies instead of fortune cookies. It read, 'Fortunes don't come true, but things you think on often do.' " Then Mom opened hers. " 'What are riches if emptiness is their price?' " She crunched into her cookie.

"Good thought," Lucy's dad said. They walked up the street.

"Hey, Lucy, let's walk by Mrs. Marshall's house and see if any numbers are crossed off the poster, shall we?" Mom suggested.

"Okay!" Maybe someone had come by during the day and offered to prepare a home for a puppy! Lucy knew they couldn't go home with their new owners yet, but she'd feel so much better when she knew loving homes were waiting for them.

They trudged up the slight hill. Lucy's dad opened his cookie.

" 'The more you look toward others, the better you feel inside.' "

He stared at Lucy.

"What?" she said, feeling uncomfortable under his gaze.

"I'm looking at you more and more so I'll feel better and better," he kidded. Lucy punched him lightly on the arm.

They passed Mrs. Marshall's house, not stopping in because they hadn't called ahead. Lucy read the sign and sighed.

Four puppies still left, and less than two days to go before the vet came and would need to be paid. And Mrs. Marshall wanted homes waiting for those dogs. It had become worse than bad. It had become impossible.

Although Lucy wanted *one* puppy left over. If only Erica would hurry.

Lucy cracked open her cookie as they walked down the hill toward their home. Her thought said, *Don't give up.*

Money Jar

Late Thursday morning . . . D Day minus one

Serena and Lucy decided to walk by and pet the pups the next day before heading over to Sweet Dreams to check on the money. Jake's mom had told them to come back on Thursday, and they were eager to see how much they'd collected. Lucy was sure it would be enough for the vet bill, now that she and her dad had both donated big. But even so, that couldn't help the pups find good homes. And even though the puppies wouldn't leave their mother for several weeks, the girls had already contacted everyone they knew to call.

They grabbed Claudette en route, promising to drop her off in a few minutes, after they had visited the pups. As the girls rounded the corner toward Mrs. Marshall's house, Serena let out a gasp. "Look!" she said.

Did she read it right? Lucy raced up to the fence where they had hung the poster. Sure enough, another number had been crossed off. It was down to three pups! The girls grabbed hands and jigged in the street.

Please don't pick little roly-poly! Lucy held to the hope that Erica would get back to her soon about keeping a puppy for Lucy for a few weeks. She didn't want to push her, though. Or maybe Erica's parents hadn't answered yet.

After pushing open the gate and walking up to the front door, Lucy knocked. Mrs. Marshall answered.

"I can see by your smile that you know my good news," Mrs. Marshall said, opening the door for Lucy, Serena, and Claudette to come in. Claudette leaned over and petted the ceramic bunnies before entering. "I told your mom this morning"—Mrs. Marshall nodded to Serena—"when she called to ask if you could come over and visit. But I told her, 'Shh. Let them find out on their own.' "

The girls ran over and saw that two of the puppies had rickrack ribbons around their necks.

"Why do some of the dogs have necklaces on?" Claudette asked, gently reaching in to stroke one of the puppies.

"When someone says they'll adopt the pup, I put a ribbon around the dog's neck. That way I can tell by the ribbon color which pup belongs to who."

Lucy sighed with relief. The little milk-splash pup didn't have a ribbon.

The girls fed the mother dog some treats. "I'm sure someone must miss this dog," Mrs. Marshall said. "She's so well trained, I just can't believe she's unwanted. But I've asked around, and no one knows who she might belong to. I hate to think of, you know, taking her over town."

Claudette clasped the mother dog to her as Mrs. Marshall said that, but no one spoke.

A good owner would have taken better care of her. I would take better care of her if she were my *dog.* Mercedes, Mrs. Marshall's dog, nudged Lucy, asking to be petted. Lucy remembered how easily Mercedes had slipped by them. Maybe this little dog had slipped by her owner on a way to an adventure, too. But this one had gotten hopelessly lost.

The girls nuzzled the dogs for a little while longer, then left to drop off Claudette back at her house.

"On to Sweet Dreams?" Serena asked, tossing her long brown-black hair in the wind.

"On to Sweet Dreams," Lucy agreed. Would she look as pretty as Serena did if she dyed her hair black?

Nah.

As they walked into the store, Jake was there to greet them. He wore a wide smile. "Guess what?" he said. "We may have found your dog's owner!"

"No!" the girls said at once.

"How? Who?" Lucy asked.

"Well, someone came into the shop and looked at the picture on the canister. He said he thought the dog might belong to one of his neighbors, but he wasn't sure. She works long hours as a hotel maid. He said her dog was missing—and he'd stay up late tonight, after her shift, to tell her about this."

Lucy and Serena looked at each other. It *was* a possibility.

"Mom told him to bring her back here tomorrow morning if her dog really was gone. Mom said she'd walk with you and the lady over to Mrs. Marshall's house when the vet comes, and she can see if it's her dog."

Like the ice cream in the case—vanilla with lumps of cookie dough mixed in—Lucy felt blended inside. Happiness with lumps of sadness mixed in. Gladness that the dog might have an owner and a good home. Sorrow that it couldn't be *her* home, not for the mother dog or any of the pups.

"Anyway, do you want to check the money?" Jake asked. "A lot of people have donated."

The girls nodded, and Jake opened the canister and shook out all of the money while the other person tended the front counter. The girls counted all of it twice. Lucy saw one hundred-dollar bill, but no others.

When the money added up, it totaled $278.25.

"That's so much!" Serena shouted. "It's enough to pay the vet bill for the mother dog and all the puppies that don't have owners." Their new families, of course, would pay for the puppies that *had* been spoken for.

Lucy grew hot inside. It was a lot. But it wasn't right. Her one hundred plus her dad's two hundred added up to three hundred dollars, plus all the money Jake had said people had contributed.

They should have way more than that.

The money must have been stolen. Just like in the old diary! But by whom?

Venus

Thursday afternoon and evening . . .

Lucy left Sweet Dreams with a restless heart. Serena was meeting her mother for a haircut, leaving Lucy to walk home alone with only her troubled thoughts for company.

Someone had stolen the money. But who? Certainly not Jake. Maybe it was that strange employee Lucy had seen behind the counter the night her dad had donated.

She felt sure that's who it was. Well, mostly sure. Not sure enough to accuse anyone . . . yet.

Lucy rounded the corner toward her house.

Maybe it wasn't that bad after all. Maybe someone— like Jake's mom—had looked in the can and thought it was dangerous to have all those hundred-dollar bills on the counter. So she was going to change them into smaller bills, or hold them till Friday.

That makes sense. I'll wait till tomorrow and see if the money's all there. If it's not, I'll have to speak up.

Her stomach squished like a jellyfish.

"Lucy! How's your new dog?" The little boy next door stumbled down the sidewalk toward her.

She smiled. "It's not my dog, Stevie. But we might have found her owner. And she's doing fine. She had puppies!"

Stevie looked up at her with wide eyes. "Puppies? Can I see them?"

Just then Lucy had her first miraculous, stupendous, awesome idea of this entire situation. Maybe *Stevie* could take a puppy.

"Stevie, I'll be right back. Don't go anywhere!" Lucy ran into her house and into the kitchen. The washing machine chugged in the laundry room, the sharp smell of laundry soap softened by the summery smell of dryer sheets. She smiled. Her mom must *almost* be caught up with the laundry by now.

"Mom? *Mom?*" she called.

Her mom peeked her head out of the refrigerator. "Nothing for dinner," she muttered. "Dead lettuce, limp carrots."

"Mom!" Lucy got her attention this time. "I have an idea."

"What is it?" her mother asked, lamenting over a stiff, overdone hamburger patty Lucy had stuffed in the butter compartment.

"Would it be okay if we asked Stevie's mother if he can have one of the puppies?"

Her mom nodded slowly. "Okay. Just a minute and I'll come over there with you."

She donated the stale food to the garbage disposal, gave it a good grind, and followed Lucy next door.

Stevie grabbed her hand and took Lucy to his mom, who sat on the covered patio out front.

"Hi!" Lucy said. Her mom stood nearby but didn't say anything.

"This is the girl who was flashing the lights on and off in her room last week," Stevie said.

Lucy's blush deepened.

"Nice to meet you."

"Well," Lucy explained. "We're helping to take care of a dog that just had puppies. The puppies aren't ready to go home yet, but we're trying to get good homes set up for them. Stevie said he always wanted a puppy, and I thought maybe you'd like to come over and see them."

Lucy stuck her hands deep in her pockets, bracing herself for the no she was used to hearing.

"Sure," Stevie's mother said.

"What did you say?" Lucy took her hands out of her pockets and clasped them together.

"I said sure. We'll come and look, at least."

Stevie jumped up and down from one foot to the other and back again.

"I'll go and call Mrs. Marshall," Lucy's mother said. Lucy bent down and played dump truck with Stevie while they waited.

"She said to come on over." Lucy's mother held the gate open for them while Stevie's mom got her keys. Then the four of them walked over to Mrs. Marshall's house. When they passed the poster, Lucy held her breath, hoping the numbers left would be *two* or *one*. But it still said *three*.

They walked up the path, and Stevie looked at the little

ceramic bunnies. The dogs weren't outside. Lucy wiped the sweat from her brow. *Summer on Catalina Island. Probably cooler inside anyway.*

Mrs. Marshall opened the door, her red curls tied back and her forehead wrapped with a purple sash.

Lucy held back a giggle. *Mrs. Marshall, martial arts wannabe. Hey—Mrs. Martial!* Lucy grinned. A gentle martial arts wannabe. It was so nice of her to keep the dogs. It was a lot of work. Mrs. Marshall had a good heart.

"This is Stevie." Lucy shepherded him in.

Stevie ran over to the pool. "Can I hold one?"

Lucy held her breath. Well, if Mrs. Marshall handed him her favorite one, Lucy would at least get to see her this summer. But Mrs. Marshall picked up another one and handed it to Stevie instead.

"This one is a little boy, like you," she said. Stevie held him for a minute, stroking the pup's fur with his stubby fingers.

Stevie didn't ask his mother if he could keep the pup, nor did he tell her that he wanted one. His mom saw it all and spoke first.

"We'll ask Stevie's dad tonight, and I'll call you. I think it will be okay, though. We've talked about getting him a pet before we have another child."

Lucy cheered that another pup had a home waiting. Especially since it wasn't little roly-poly.

"Want to put a ribbon around your puppy's neck?" Mrs. Marshall asked.

Stevie picked out a yellow ribbon—the color of his dump truck. Mrs. Marshall tied it loosely around his pup's neck. She explained about their paying for the vet and the pet food. Stevie's mother didn't seem to mind.

Lucy rubbed behind the mother dog's ears and spoke softly to her. "Your owner might be coming tomorrow, girl. I hope it's her, if she's nice to you. I'd like to keep you myself, but I can't. And you belong with your owner."

She reached over and petted the two pups with no ribbons. No homes for them. And tomorrow was Friday.

Maybe one of them would be for her.

She stood up and noticed her mother speaking quietly in the corner with Mrs. Marshall. After Lucy came near, they finished off their conversation, and then Lucy and her mom walked home with Stevie and his mother.

☂ ☂ ☂

Late that night, Lucy and her parents took a ride in a borrowed Jeep, which the Island government kept for research purposes. They drove back into the interior of the Island so her dad could observe some night-blooming flowers. Lucy loved nighttime drives. It reminded her of the times when they'd all pile into the car and take hot chocolate and drive to look at Christmas lights.

But last Christmas, her parents were separated. There had been no Christmas rides.

So now Lucy smiled and settled in for the last minutes of the ride. She watched her parents talk in the front seat. Maybe they were driving away from those troubles for good.

Not just anyone was allowed into the interior of the

Island. Tourists could visit Avalon and Two Harbors, the other dot-sized town on Catalina Island. But you had to have a special card to open the one and only gate guarding the road to the Island interior.

Lucy's dad pulled his university-issued card from his wallet and ran it through the gate. The gate opened, and they drove through. The cover was off of the Jeep, so there was nothing between Lucy and the night except the Jeep's roll bar and a warm, sweet breeze. Lucy held on, watching the dry, rocky ground blur past her till they got to her dad's observing area.

Her mom and dad got out to take some samples and a picture.

Lucy opened up a lawn chair and set it in the middle of the desert, surrounded by quiet and cactus. She opened up a cold Dr Pepper and stared at the stars.

Way out there, yet still inside her somehow, was God. God, who put all the stars in a pattern, the pattern He wanted them in. Some of those stars made cool patterns when you looked at them together. Lucy grabbed her Star Finder and looked up. Libra was there, so was Scorpio.

Lucy remembered when she'd gotten her first dog, Jupiter, and her promise to name all of her pets after the planets. She scanned the ecliptic, the train track for the sun, moon, and stars. It was a little late at night, but she thought she saw bright, white Venus.

Venus was strange. It rotated backward.

Lucy giggled. Kind of like the little roly-poly fuzzy pup. Always rolling backward. *You can tell what's on my mind.*

Before leaving the house that night, Lucy had tried to

call Erica to see if Erica's parents had answered about the puppy. But no one was home.

"Back for another prayer, Lord," Lucy whispered into the sky that seemed open to her whispered plea. "Thanks for everything you've done so far. Thank you for my friends—and my family." She looked at her parents, working together. "Both my mom and dad and the new family I'm just starting to know—other Christians. But tomorrow is Friday, there are two puppies left, and money is missing. Please help me to be able to keep roly-poly. Amen."

Mrs. Beppo

Friday morning . . . D Day!

When her alarm went off at 8:41 A.M., Lucy woke up. She'd been wandering between asleep and awake for some time, so she rolled over and turned the beeper off right away.

D Day.

She ran into the bathroom and hopped under a quick shower, running clean hands through her tangle of curly red-gold hair afterward to straighten it out. Then she jazzed back into her room, thinking of what she could wear. They'd stop at Sweet Dreams first to see how much money was there, and to see if the dog's owner showed up.

I hope all the money is back in the can.

Lucy picked out a gold shirt, which made her hair seem even shinier, and a pair of black shorts. Her mood ring and her turquoise ring sat on her night table; she slipped them over her knuckles and put on her wire necklace.

Lucy grabbed the old diary and her and Serena's friendship diary, then walked down for breakfast. They'd kind of forgotten about the diary till now. And today they'd have to write in it—success or failure!

"Sleeping in?" her mother asked. Lucy looked up. Her mom looked really pretty today. The sun had warmed her skin over the past few weeks and her smile seemed light.

"Yeah," Lucy answered. "But I'm ready to go and see the dogs."

"Serena's coming over in half an hour, right?" Mom said. "So you've got some time to eat."

"Uh-huh," Lucy mumbled. She dished up some fruit and dabbed a smudge of cream cheese on half a bagel. She pushed around a few pieces of melon and finally popped a banana slice into her mouth. Picking through the rest, she found the starfruit, then munched part of her bagel.

After running upstairs to brush her teeth, Lucy sat by the front door, waiting.

Finally Serena rang the bell.

"Bye, Mom! See you at Mrs. Marshall's!" she called.

She opened the door and hugged Serena. Just as they got down to the sidewalk, Lucy remembered. *The envelopes!*

"Wait here!" she said to Serena. She ran back into the house, up the stairs, and into her room. She pulled open her desk drawer and reached in. The envelopes she'd filled just a couple of days ago still rested there. She snuck them into her woven shoulder bag and ran back down the stairs.

Then she and Serena headed toward Sweet Dreams.

"What do you think is going to happen?" Serena asked.

"With what?"

"You know, the dog's owner . . . and everything."

The way Serena said "and everything" sounded strange to Lucy. Serena couldn't possibly mean the missing money. She didn't know about it. Lucy just shrugged her shoulders.

As they rounded the corner, Lucy tucked her gold shirt in and hoped she looked as cute as Serena always did. Today Serena had on a red shirt that looked great with her dark hair.

They opened the door to the ice-cream shop and saw an older woman sitting in a chair in the corner.

"Is Jake here?" Lucy asked the person at the counter. The boy walked into the back, and Jake and his mom came out.

"Mrs. Beppo has been waiting for you," Jake's mom whispered as she glanced at the old lady in the corner chair. Mrs. Beppo clutched her purse.

Lucy's heart softened as she looked at the elderly woman. The girls walked straight over to her, with Jake and his mother right behind. Mrs. Beppo's face had soft wrinkles, folding around her eyes to make them little green diamonds. A soft old-lady mustache shadowed her upper lip.

"I'm Lucy." Lucy sat in the chair next to Mrs. Beppo so they'd be at the same eye level. "My friend Serena and I found a little lost dog. Do you think it might be yours?"

Mrs. Beppo's eyes filled with tears. "It might be. My Misty escaped last weekend. You see, I'm a hotel maid, and I had to work a double shift."

"That means she worked sixteen hours in a row," Jake's mom said softly.

Lucy looked at Serena. An old lady who had to clean hotel rooms for sixteen hours in a row!

"I didn't want to leave Misty in the house all that time. So I hooked her leash to a stake and put her in the grassy area in back of my townhouse. When I got home, her collar was attached to the leash, but Misty was gone."

She dabbed her eyes. "She does look like the dog on your can. And she was ready to have puppies. Though I don't know how I'm going to pay for *that*."

Lucy reached over and touched the old lady's arm. "I think we may have found Misty, and she did have some puppies this week. But don't worry, the vet bill has been taken care of." She explained about the canister of money.

The old lady smiled. "My neighbor came in and saw the canister and the sign. He recognized my dog and came to tell me. I . . . I don't have a lot of money for things like ice cream. So I don't visit ice-cream shops."

Lucy thought back to Saturday, when they had read the old diary, and how people walked by with ice cream all the time. She remembered thinking that no one on this island went without.

She was wrong.

She leaned over to Jake and whispered in his ear. Jake nodded and spoke up.

"Would you like an ice-cream cone before we go?" Jake asked Mrs. Beppo.

Mrs. Beppo's tired eyes crinkled with delight. "Oh yes, please. I would love a cone. Rocky Road, if you have it. But, please, I'm also eager to see my dog."

Jake went over to scoop her a waffle-cone sundae, and Serena and Lucy stood up when they saw Amy and Erica walk into the store.

The four girls huddled in the corner. "Guys, if there is money left over—" Lucy swallowed—"and we don't know if there is yet—I think we should give it to Mrs. Beppo. If Misty is her dog, she seems like she needs some help buying dog food and stuff."

The other three girls nodded their approval. Now, if Lucy only knew how much money she was going to find in the can.

Mrs. Beppo polished off her cone as fast as Stevie would have and grinned with pleasure. "Thank you, young man," she said. "I enjoyed that very much."

Jake's mom picked up the canister and held it close. "I think we should be going."

Lucy had planned to count the money before they left the store. But she wasn't going to snatch the can from Jake's mother.

The girls gathered up their things, and Jake and his mother walked Mrs. Beppo out the door. For an old lady, she was remarkably strong.

They all headed up the street toward Mrs. Marshall's house.

"So you say the puppies have been born," Mrs. Beppo said. "I love puppies." Her eyes crinkled with delight again.

A shot of fear ran through Lucy's arms as she had a new and frightening thought. She leaned over and whispered to Serena, "What if Mrs. Beppo wants to keep all the puppies, or give them to *her* friends, and we've already promised three of them to other people? Then we'd have to tell Stevie and Roger and the other family. And then there won't be enough money to pay for the vet, which we already promised to do!"

And then I won't have one to keep at Erica's house, either, Lucy thought.

Serena's eyes opened wide. "I hadn't thought of that. And it's much worse than that."

"What do you mean? What?"

Just then they arrived in front of Mrs. Marshall's house, and Lucy saw the poster. All the numbers were crossed off. *All* of the puppies had been promised.

Lucy stood there, frozen, in front of the sign.

Erica hadn't asked soon enough, and now all the puppies were taken! Anger crossed through Lucy.

Jake's mom spoke up. "Well? Shall we go in?"

The girls moved past the ceramic bunnies and knocked on Mrs. Marshall's door.

Just Between Friends

Friday noon . . .

Mrs. Marshall answered the door. "Come on in!" Lucy and the girls stepped aside to let Mrs. Beppo in first. Mrs. Beppo's face broke into a giant smile, and she ran over to the mother dog.

"Mia cara!" She embraced the dog. Misty leaped up, leaving her pups, and jumped toward Mrs. Beppo. Mrs. Beppo held out her hands and cuddled the dog.

Lucy smiled. "I guess it's her dog, all right," she said.

Lucy's mom and dad had already arrived and stood near the back of the room, chatting together. Lucy waved to them, and Jake's mother went to stand with them.

"I've examined them, and they seem fine," the vet said. "The pups will have to stay with the mother for several weeks, then they can go to their new homes."

New homes. Lucy decided to speak up.

"Mrs. Beppo?" she said. "We've found good homes for the puppies." Lucy remembered the poster board that read zero, although she'd noticed that two of the pups didn't have ribbons around their necks. "We didn't know if the dog—I mean, Misty—had an owner or not. But do you plan to keep the puppies, too?"

Lucy held her breath. Everyone else seemed to, as well.

"The puppies?" Mrs. Beppo said. "No. If you've found good homes for them, it's just as well. I can barely afford to keep Misty."

The vet spoke up. "I'd be glad to talk with you about operating on Misty later so she won't have any more puppies."

He must have seen the alarmed look in Mrs. Beppo's eyes. "Free of charge," he generously offered. The room erupted in smiles all around.

The vet spoke to the four girls, who huddled together, though Lucy stood farthest away from Erica. "I'm really impressed with you young ladies. You've found good homes for all of these dogs, and that's not easy to do." He grinned. "Well done. And now, I need to sign off on all of their ownership certificates. If someone could please hand me the stack on that table one by one, I'll sign them now."

"You do it, Lucy," Erica said. She smiled, and Lucy smiled back.

"Okay." Lucy stepped forward and took the stack of ownership certificates. She handed him the one with Roger's family's name on it and a little strip of ribbon the same color as the one around his puppy's neck.

Then she handed over Stevie's, with the yellow ribbon attached. The vet signed off that he had examined the pup and the date he'd be back to give the first set of shots.

Next came the pup that had been adopted by the first family who had seen Erica's poster.

When Lucy came to the fourth certificate she read out loud, " 'Lucy Larson.' " Then she handed over the certificate. Her throat tightened.

"LUCY LARSON?" she shouted, "ME?"

Everyone in the room laughed. Goose bumps rose on Lucy's arms and prickled down her back. "How can that be?"

Her dad gave her a little squeeze and stepped forward. "We knew how much you wanted a dog, so I called the university and asked them if we might have a pet. I offered to send them a damage deposit of two hundred dollars in case the dog scratched or chewed anything. They called back and agreed."

Lucy ran back to the puppies. The little roly-poly milk-splash one still had no ribbon on her neck. Lucy nuzzled her close.

She spoke to Mrs. Marshall. "Is this one promised yet?"

"Yes," Mrs. Marshall said. "To you."

Lucy reached in and stroked little Venus. She whispered, "You're mine, girl. I'll always be here for you."

Then she stood up. "But how did you know this was the one I wanted?"

Her mother smiled. "I called Serena and asked her which one you liked best, and she told me. I asked Mrs. Marshall to save her for last, till we were really sure the university would agree to our proposal with the damage deposit." Lucy felt sad that she had hugged and thanked her dad so naturally, but it hadn't come as easy between her and her mom. She reached up and kissed her cheek.

Lucy looked at Serena. "You knew all along!"

Serena grinned. "Hoped, not knew. No one knew till the university called your dad back, and even I wasn't sure till I saw the zero on the sign today. But Erica and Amy were praying with me."

Lucy said, "You guys! Keeping a secret from me!" She ran to hug Erica, who had known all along but hadn't wanted to give the secret away.

Erica spoke up, echoing Lucy's comment the other day when Mercedes had gotten loose. "What's a little secret when it's just between friends?"

"The last certificate!" Lucy spoke up. The vet had already signed it. Lucy picked it up and read the name.

"Claudette Kingsley!" She beamed. "Does Claudette know yet?"

"No," her mom said. "We thought you might want to be there when we told her. We can go over later this afternoon."

Lucy grabbed a Dr Pepper–colored ribbon and tied it around Venus's neck. Then she grabbed two pieces of ribbon—one orange and one pink—and tied them around the last pup.

"Why two ribbons?" Serena asked.

"To match Claudette's socks," Lucy said, smiling. The other girls smiled, too.

Lucy took the canister from Jake's mom.

I'm so glad I didn't accuse anyone of stealing money. Dad didn't put two hundred dollars in there after all. He'd planned to send it to the university.

She opened the canister and paid the vet, then handed the rest to Mrs. Beppo.

"We wanted to give you the rest to buy dog food. And," she said with a twinkle, "some ice cream whenever you want."

Mrs. Beppo leaned over and kissed Lucy on the cheek.

"We'd better go," Erica said. She and Amy headed for the door.

"Wait!" Lucy called out. She reached into her woven bag and handed them each an envelope with each girl's name on it. "Open it at home, okay?"

The girls nodded, turning the envelopes over in their hands, looking for a clue, maybe.

Lucy walked over to her parents and pulled them into a corner.

"Serena and I are going to the beach to read the rest of the diary, okay?"

Her parents nodded, and she pulled them close so no one else could hear. "Thanks for showing me how to ask for help without feeling like I'm a bad person if I can't think of everything on my own."

Her dad had a questioning look on his face. "What do you mean?"

"The marriage class," Lucy whispered.

Mom and Dad grinned.

Then Lucy and Serena walked to the beach, the old diary and the new diary in Lucy's bag.

"So do I get one of those envelopes, too?" Serena teased.

"Yeeeeessss," Lucy said. "Be patient!"

The two of them ran to the beach and popped open the yellow umbrella at their special spot.

Serena opened the diary and began to read.

"We're back, dear diary, and here is some good news. Someone did steal the money, at least that's the best that we can figure. But hear this—the whole town was so outraged that they came together and donated three times as much as the stolen money! The church led the collection drive, but everyone pitched in."

The writing changed and Lucy began to read.

"So, the poor will be fed, at least for now, and we'll get to help as the summer goes on."

Serena cut in, "We got to help, too, though we didn't know how that was going to happen at first, did we?"

Lucy looked over the shimmering sand and out into the clear blue water. She turned to Serena and smiled. "You know what? We did help a dog, and her puppies. But most important, we helped people. Like Mrs. Beppo." She thought of Mrs. Beppo, an older lady, working so many hours and still not having too much. "And there are poor people all around us, whether we see them or not."

"We helped you, too," Serena said softly. "No more crying over Jupiter. Venus is in orbit."

Lucy smiled. "Yes, she is."

Lucy turned back to the diary and read:

"Well, diary, we've got quite a dare ahead of us this next week. Both of us are a bit afraid of what lies ahead, but we're going to press on in spite of our fear. Till then, Mary and Serena. Faithful friends."

Lucy's eyes opened wide. "They're *both* afraid this time?"

Serena clutched her stomach. "No more trouble. *Please!*"

Lucy giggled. "She didn't say trouble, she said *fear*."

"Worse!" Serena said.

Lucy laughed and reached back into her bag. "Here, maybe this will help keep your mind off it till tomorrow." She handed over the envelope with Serena's name on it.

Serena slit open the envelope and drew out a paper doll—three dolls connected, holding hands. The doll to the right had a dress on, and Lucy had colored in black hair and on the bottom wrote *Serena*. The doll to the left had a dress on, too, and Lucy had colored in strawberry-blond hair. At the bottom she'd written *Lucy*. In the middle was a man, the dress snipped away to make pants. Lucy had drawn in manly hair and a beard. At the bottom was written *Jesus*.

"He should always be between friends," Lucy said.

Serena looked at it and said, "Let's slip it into our diary. Forever."

Lucy took out their *own* best friends' diary, and they wrote together.

Fearful things tomorrow, diary. Fear, Lucy wrote, teasing Serena. *And Serena's got a tummy ache about it.*

We'll see who's got a tummy ache after tomorrow, diary, Serena wrote. *But let me tell you how this week worked out.*

Then Lucy and Serena took turns writing about that week's adventure. Serena drew a little sketch of Venus, puppy wonder.

They signed off, as always:

Faithful Friends.

For where two or three gather together
because they are mine,
I am there among them.

MATTHEW 18:20 (NLT)

SANDRA BYRD and her family love pets. Things got too quiet and lonely when their dog, Trudy, had to go away to train for 4-H and live on a ranch for a while. So Sandra and her family adopted a kitten named Charlotte, who will live at Sandra's house forever.

Sandra lives near beautiful Seattle, between snow-capped Mount Rainier and the Space Needle, with her husband and two children. When she's not writing, she's usually reading, but she also likes to scrapbook, listen to music, and spend time with friends. Besides writing THE HIDDEN DIARY books, she's also the author of the bestselling series SECRET SISTERS.

For more information on THE HIDDEN DIARY series, visit Sandra's Web site: *www.thehiddendiary.com.* Or you can write to Sandra at

Sandra Byrd
P.O. Box 1207
Maple Valley, WA 98038

**Don't miss book four
of THE HIDDEN DIARY,
*Take a Bow!***

For a preview of Lucy and Serena's next diary adventure, just hold up this page in front of a mirror.

It's time for the Island Art Fair. Lucy thinks it'll be great fun. But when she is asked to face her biggest fear, she quickly changes her tune.